YOUNG ASSASSIN

A novel by MIKE "G"

A Life Changing Book in conjunction with Power Play Media
Published by Life Changing Books
P.O. Box 423 Brandywine, MD 20613

Library of Congress Cataloging-in-Publication Data;

www.lifechangingbooks.net

ISBN - (10) 1-934230-98-7 (13) 978-1-934230-98-5
Copyright ® 2007

Dedications

This book is dedicated to the loving memories of my grandmother, Cora Evans, my father, Louis Grayson, and my uncle, Sergeant John Colquitt, Sr. Thank you for your unconditional love and all of the warm memories that will last a lifetime. You will always be in my heart.

I also commit this book to the elevation of today's young generation. It's far better to walk the straight and narrow path than the path that leads to self-destruction. Be a leader and not a follower.

Acknowledgements

First and foremost, I want to thank the Creator of Heaven and Earth. Without Him, I can do nothing, and with Him, I can do anything. Thank You for Your help and strength, Almighty God, and thank You for maintaining and sustaining me. Whatever You have in store for me, I will be truly grateful, and whatever obstacles lie ahead, I will call on You and pray that You will hearken onto me in my prayers.

Mom, thank you so much for everything you've done for me. Since I was a youngster, I always dreamed of being an author. You've been with me the entire way. From when I first started writing, and throughout my ordeals with callous literary agents until now, I thank you for believing in me and being by my side every step of the way.

To Tyrone and Archie, my older brothers, thank you for providing me with the pure example and guidance on how to be a man. The two of you are vital components that equal into the man I am today. If I were born before you two, I truly don't think I would've been wise enough to deal with the world, or be a big brother to you as both of you have been to me. Luckily, I was born after you!

To all of my friends, family and colleagues who have shown me support, I can never give enough thanks. There's too many to name, but thank you for purchasing a copy of my novel.

I would like to give a shout out to RAW SISTAZ, and to Miss Missy of APOOO Book Club. To Michele Leslie, and Collective Voices, thank you so much for having me on your program. To Ebony Eyes Book Club in B-More, to Lovely Lisa, Pam, Lauren, Tanya, Dawn, Rita, Kim, Debra, Katasha, Jackie, Rhonda, Jeanette, Ja'Meda, Chekevia, C. Tamara, Eric Jr., and Mike Jr., thank you for having me at your book club meetings. I truly cherished the great experience, the warm hospitality, and the delicious food. I hope to visit you again in the future.

To Professor Art Jones, you were there encouraging me from the beginning. I think I was barely twenty-one years old when we met and gave you my first ever manuscript to read over. That seems like eons ago. Even when things looked impossible, you kept inspiring me with hope. Thank you for being a mentor, a brother, and a friend.

To Azarel, author of *A Life To Remember, Bruised and Bruised 2*. I don't know where to even begin. It seems that even saying thank you isn't enough. Thank you for taking on my project, and helping me make my dreams come true. Because of you, a lot of people will be reading my book. I can't express my gratitude enough. Thank you again!

Thank you to the group of professionals who worked on this project. Kathleen Jackson, thanks for your dedication and expertise on editing my work. Leslie Allen, thanks for your technical support. Nakea Murray, thanks for wearing many, many hats. Vida, the book cover is awesome!!

Shout out to all the other authors with Life Changing Books and Power Play Media. J. Tremble (More Secrets More Lies; Secrets of a Housewife), Tonya Ridley (The Takeover), Tyrone Wallace (Nothin' Personal; Double Life) Danette Majette (I Shoulda Seen It Comin'), Tiphani Montgomery (The Millionaire Mistress), and Darren Coleman (Do or Die; Ladies Listen Up). 2007 will be a good year for us!

Thanks to all the distributors, Baker & Taylor, Ingram, Lushena, Borders, African World Books, and Karibu. Your support is greatly appreciated.

To Doc, (R.I.P). I still mourn you until this day.

~Mike G.

1986

Chapter One

Just as he was about to sit on his bed, young Maurice jumped at the sound of the four heavy knocks at the front door. With his clipboard in hand, he jetted downstairs, hoping it wasn't the police inquiring about Lemar again.

"Who is it?" Maurice asked, moving closer to the door. Strangely, there was no answer. Maurice frowned. He backed up a few steps, debating whether he should open the door.

"Who's there?" he asked again. He walked to the door and reached for the knob, but before he could even touch it, the glass window in the living room shattered, and a huge red brick came flying through.

Maurice dropped the clipboard and ran upstairs, with fear in his heart.

"We need to hurry up before somebody sees us!" a voice yelled from outside.

Maurice made it to his mother's room, shut the door, and rushed over to the window. A few seconds later, he heard a loud commotion downstairs. *Oh snap, they're inside,* he thought. He tried desperately to pull up the window, but it wouldn't go up.

"That little niggah got to be in here somewhere. Let's go find his ass!" the same voice from outside shouted.

"I just heard a noise upstairs. He's probably up there!" another voice stated.

Young Assassin

Maurice dashed over to his mother's jewelry box that was on top of her dresser, and searched desperately for the skeleton key to lock the bedroom door, but he couldn't find it anywhere. When he heard footsteps coming up the stairs, he knew his time was running out.

"Damn," he whispered to himself. "Somebody, please help me."

A tear slid down his face as he began to panic. He looked for anything he could grab to use as a weapon. Maurice's head moved back and forth, as his eyes tried to locate something.

By now, the intruders had made it upstairs and were in the hallway. He knew it would be less than five seconds before they found him. Suddenly, he spotted his mother's iron lying on the floor by the closet door. He quickly walked over and grabbed it.

At that moment, the door flew open, and four men rushed inside. Maurice charged at the first man he saw, with the iron cocked back. He hit the man on the side of the head and tried to make a run for the door, but two other men forcefully body-slammed him to the floor. He kicked, clawed and fought them, trying to get loose.

"Try not to hurt the boy." The voice carried a strange European accent.

Maurice tried to fight, but it was no use. The man who told his companions not to hurt him stepped closer.

"Who are you? What do you want?" Maurice questioned, frowning as he struggled in the strong clutches of the two men.

"My name is Sebastian, and we came for you."

Sebastian looked down at the guy who Maurice had hit upside the head with the iron. There was a nasty looking gash on the side of his head, and blood gushed onto the pink carpet.

Sebastian gazed into Maurice face, and said, "Now cooperate, and we'll be friends. Insubordination could result in your death."

Maurice shook his head as the man he hit stumbled to his

feet. "Leave me alone," he said. "I haven't done anything to you punks."

Sebastian laughed. "This isn't personal, I assure you. Now, are you going to cooperate, or do we have to do things the hard way?"

Maurice struggled once more, as Sebastian's tall, hefty frame stepped into his face. Finally, Maurice sighed and slumped his shoulders in defeat. "What do you want from me?" he asked.

"You'll find out soon enough," Sebastian said.

He reached into the pocket of his black leather jacket and grabbed a sock, which he smashed into Maurice's nose, and held it there with all the force he could muster.

Maurice's slim, one hundred pound body, became drowsy as he breathed in the fumes of a solid vapor. He rallied as much strength as he could, but his body began to fail him. He coughed and struggled to hold up his head. Suddenly, his eyes closed, and his head pointed south, like a jet taking a nosedive into the ground.

Sebastian removed the sock and placed it back into his coat pocket. He looked at the two men holding Maurice up. "Hurry up and get him into the van," he said.

Lemar traveled Uptown to his dormitory on the campus of Howard University. He hardly ever stayed there, except when he needed time to think. Lemar knew he should've been focusing on school, but the money he got from the street outweighed his education.

He parked his car near the campus, and walked about two hundred yards to his dorm. He went inside and ran up the three flights of stairs to his room. When Lemar entered, he turned on the light and looked at the place. It had a twin-sized bed that he'd left unmade, and a seventeen-inch color television. There were a few plants next to a closet door, that his mother had given him when he first moved in, which looked as if they'd died weeks ago.

Lemar paced back and forth, thinking about the dilemma with his coke supplier. He scrutinized things as deeply as he could, trying to judge it with pure justice. In the midst of being wanted on drug charges, he also had to face an important crisis. He either had to compensate his supplier with thousands of dollars, or possibly go to war. The other option was to just turn himself in, but Lemar was smart enough to know he couldn't hide, even in prison. His back was up against the wall, and he had to come out swinging. After careful examination, Lemar came up with an answer. *I don't owe that niggah shit,* he thought. *What went down wasn't even my fault.*

Just then, he thought of his mother and little brother, and also wondered about Seth, his good friend who was still locked up. They both had been set up by their long-time friend, Martin Reed, but Lemar had managed to elude the police.

There's a thin line between friend and foe, Lemar thought, and if Martin were to ever get out of jail, he knew somebody would try to kill him.

He became sleepy as his worries started to die down a bit. He'd been up all morning, trying to get his head together. With the prospect of having to turn himself in, and the constant threats from his supplier, Lemar had his hands full.

by Mike C

Loretta parked her car on her residential block, and sat in it for a while thinking. She had just come from a church service, after putting in eight hours at work. She finally got out, wearing the white mink coat her ex-husband had given her years ago, and walked slowly up the sidewalk, humming a spiritual song.

When she reached the house, she saw several D.C. policemen standing on the porch. She stopped and stared at them, with a confused look on her face. "Can I help you?" she asked.

"Is this your house?" one of the policemen asked.

Loretta nodded. "Yes. Is there something wrong?"

At that moment, Maurice's short, chubby friend named J.B., ran up to her, and grabbed her hand. "Ms. Patterson, I called the police when I noticed your window was broken!" he said. "I think someone broke into your house."

Her gaze shifted from her son's friend to the policemen occupying her porch. "My house got broken into? My window is busted?"

"I'm afraid so," the same policeman said. "We've been awaiting your arrival for over an hour. We'd like to go inside and look around."

"Oh, Jesus," she said, putting a hand on her forehead and closing her eyes. She'd been in a pleasant mood until now.

Loretta opened her eyes and stepped up on the porch. When she looked back, J.B. was staring at her like his favorite food. Loretta unlocked the door and went inside, as the policemen followed. She turned on the living room light, and saw that the window over the radiator had been shattered.

"Someone definitely broke inside this place," the over-sized police officer uttered. "Oh, please forgive me, I'm Officer Bailey," he said. He looked down and picked up a drawing attached to a clipboard. "There's a huge shoe print on top of this drawing."

Loretta looked at him. "What?"

5

"Who's Maurice Patterson?" Officer Bailey asked, looking at the signature on the bottom of the paper. His expression changed instantly.

"My son," Loretta said, looking at what the cop had come across. "He was here alone. Oh my God, I hope he's okay."

"Are you Lemar Patterson's mother?" Officer Bailey asked.

"Yes, but what does that have to do with Maurice?"

Two of the policemen instantly pulled their guns, and headed upstairs to search for anything strange. The other two cops remained downstairs with Loretta.

"Bailey, can you come up here?" one of the policemen asked.

Officer Bailey turned and headed up the stairs. Loretta tried to follow, but he stopped her in a polite manner. "There's no telling what the officers may have found up there," he said. "It could be really bad."

She swallowed. "Like my son's body?"

"Precisely," Bailey said, with a smirk. He looked at the other policemen in the living room. "Go down to the basement and see what you can find."

Bailey hurried upstairs to check out what was going on in Loretta's room. Her jewelry box was turned sideways, and large spots of blood were on the rug. They were particularly interested in the iron laying in the middle of the floor with dried blood on it.

"Ma'am, you can come upstairs now!" Bailey yelled.

Loretta slowly walked upstairs, afraid of what she'd see. Immediately, she looked at her jewelry box. All her rings, chains, and the rest of her stuff were there. Her eyes became huge, as she noticed the iron.

"Jesus," she said, extending one of her hands into the air, as she placed the other one over her heart. Loretta stood there, thinking of her son. "What does this look like to you?" she asked Bailey.

6

Just then, one of the other officers interrupted, "We're through in the basement. Everything appears to be normal down there."

Bailey looked at Loretta, who had a facial expression that asked a thousand questions. "I believe someone may have abducted your son," he said, with confidence. "We're gonna need to ask you some more questions, and until we get to the bottom of this, I think it's best if you find a safe place to stay. Is that possible?"

Loretta gazed deeply into Bailey's mouth, noticing how shiny his braces gleamed. "Yes," she responded. "I can stay with my mother." She slowly walked toward her nightstand. "Please, Good Jehovah, don't let anything happen to my boy," she said, picking up the receiver. As Loretta waited for her mother to answer, she wondered why this was happening. Suddenly, it all clicked, she knew there could only be one reason, Lemar. She had put him out a little over a year ago. Yet somehow he'd managed to still bring karma back to the house. "Help me, Jesus!" she shouted.

❊ ❊ ❊

When Maurice came to, he felt cold and had a slight headache. He tried to move his hands, but they were tied behind his back and to his feet with some kind of rope. His mouth was gagged, and he lay in a curled position on the floor, trying to free himself.

Where am I? His mind raced with thoughts, and then he suddenly remembered something. He'd been at home drawing a picture of his brother, Lemar, when he heard knocks on the front door, and then a brick smashing through the living room window. He was then body-slammed and remembered some fool named

Sebastian, who had a strange English accent. That was all his mind would allow him to recall.

The answer to where he was remained unknown, but now he realized he'd been kidnapped. Why he was kidnapped, he had no idea. The winter cold from outside caused him to shiver. The temperature in the pitch-black room had to be at least fifteen to twenty degrees, and the thin Coca-Cola shirt he wore, didn't provide much warmth.

Maurice took a deep breath. The frigid air entered his nostrils and traveled down into his lungs. He held his breath for a few seconds, before letting it back out. He rolled over to where he thought a wall would be, hoping to find a door. He slithered on his side, brushing his hands against the walls of the room until he felt metal.

This has got to be a door, he thought. He knew the knob had to be just above him. He tried with every bit of strength to break free, but the rope was too strong and tied too securely for him to get out of the uncomfortable position.

Suddenly, he heard the sound of footsteps from somewhere nearby, as he looked at the darkness in front of him. The steps became louder, and Maurice became even more frightened. He slid from in front of the door and back into the middle of the dark room. The steps came to a halt, and he heard the sound of a door closing. Suddenly, the light was turned on. Maurice squinted his eyes, as the bright light from the ceiling shined down on him.

He looked up and saw a petite woman with short, sandy-brown hair, and slanted eyes, resembling an Asian woman. She wore a Nike sweatsuit underneath an opened brown leather trench coat, and python-skin boots. She smiled as she walked toward him with a coffee cup.

Maurice looked around the room. It was completely empty, with the exception of several roaches that ran across the four dirty white walls. He immediately searched for a window, but there wasn't one.

"I brought you some hot chocolate," the woman said, in a warm voice.

She walked over to him and put the cup on the floor, then untied the tight cloth from around his mouth and stared at him. Maurice returned the look. "Who are you? What am I doing here?

Where am I?" he asked the woman, as soon as she removed the cloth from his mouth.

"My name is Alvina," she told him. "My fiancé took a drastic measure and had you abducted because of a debt your brother, Lemar, owes him. It's nothing personal. Just business."

"Does my brother know where I am?"

"I don't think so," Alvina said. "Besides, if he did, you'd be free by now."

Alvina reached for the cup of hot chocolate and put it up to his lips. He looked at her for a moment, before allowing her to give it to him.

"This will warm you up," she said.

Hesitantly, Maurice drank, tasting the rich chocolate flavor as it went down his throat. He took three more swallows before turning his head.

"I want to go home," he said, in a childish tone.

"All in due time," Alvina replied, as she held the cup to his lips again. "You want some more?" she asked.

"Why did you come here?" Maurice asked, before taking a few more swallows.

"Doug sent me," she said.

"Who's Doug?"

"My fiancé. He's the one your brother owes the debt to." She smiled.

"So, is Doug gonna kill me?" Maurice responded, with a worried expression.

Her smile disappeared. "I doubt it. This is just to let Lemar

know Doug wants his money, and that he's not playing around."
She placed the cup on the floor. "Well, I gotta go," she said, putting the cloth back around his mouth. Luckily for him, she didn't tie it tight.

Maurice looked down at her python-skin boots, and stared her up and down. She was fine, and if the situation were different, he'd definitely have a crush on her.

Alvina displayed another beautiful smile. "I'll bring you something to eat later on tonight." She picked up the cup of hot chocolate, turned off the light switch, and headed out the room.

Maurice was alone in the dark once again. He heard her put the lock on the door, and the sounds of her brusque footsteps moved farther and farther away. He sighed and began to think about his mother, Lemar, and if he'd live to see another day.

Chapter Two

Doug sat in his living room, with Sebastian on the comfort-
able black leather sofa. His large twelve-foot boa constrictor was
wrapped around his shoulders, as he sat in deep thought.
Sebastian held a glass of 151 rum mixed with cola in his hand,
while Doug chose to drink a tall glass of orange juice instead.

Doug got up and walked to his room. He came back out a
minute later with a kilo of cocaine, and handed it to Sebastian.

"Here's your reward for gettin' a hold of Lemar's brother."

"Thanks a lot, old friend," Sebastian said. "The kid actually
managed to hurt one of my men." He put the drink to his lips and
took a few sips. "Why didn't you go after Lemar anyway?"

Doug's smile turned into a devilish grin. "I like Lemar," he
replied, taking a seat beside Sebastian. "I just want him to know
I'm not fucking around, that's all. He'll take me more seriously
this way."

Suddenly, the front door opened, and Alvina came in. She
removed her coat and tossed it on the loveseat.

"How's the boy?" Doug asked.

"He's cold, hungry and scared, Doug. Don't forget, he's only
fifteen. How would you feel if someone had you tied up in the
basement of a crack house?"

Doug placed the snake on the floor to give it freedom. "I'm a
soldier, so it wouldn't bother me."

"You're taking your business too personal," she replied.

Doug stood up and walked over to his girl. His face displayed
a threatening look, as their eyes met.

"Don't ever tell me how to conduct business. Do you understand?"

Alvina shook her head. "No, Doug, I don't."

In a flash, he raised his hand and swung toward her face. Alvina weaved to the side, making Doug cleanly miss. "Let's not do this," she said, walking away from him.

"How can you speak with such disloyalty?" Doug asked, following her, like he had a score to settle.

"I've always been loyal to you," Alvina responded. "I just disagree with how you're handling this."

"And how's that?" He got in her face. "Give me an explanation."

"Come on, Doug!" she said, raising her voice. "Kidnapping a harmless boy because his brother is missing a few kilos of coke? That's ridiculous! And that wasn't even Lemar's fault! You know he got robbed. Do you even realize you can get ten to fifteen years in jail for that stupid shit? You need to cut them some slack."

There was a tone in her voice that Doug didn't appreciate. He took another swing at her, and this time, caught her dead on the cheek. Alvina's knees buckled, but she managed to keep from falling. She placed a hand on the side of her face, and stared at him in rage, as she struggled to keep herself calm.

"Money is money. Lemar should've been armed, as well as the guys he was dealing with. This is his karma. Now his little brother is paying for his incompetence," Doug said, with anger in his eyes.

Alvina backed up a couple steps and walked around him. Doug kept an eye on her, as she walked into his bedroom and slammed the door.

"Man, why did you hit her?" Sebastian asked.

"She needs to learn how to stay in her place," Doug replied, as his anger died down. He walked back to the sofa, grabbed the glass of orange juice off the coffee table, and took a few sips.

❄ ❄ ❄

Lemar woke up in the middle of the night, after getting some rest. He sat up, looked around, and then remembered he was in his dorm room. He yawned as he rubbed his temples. His pager began to beep. Lemar reached into the brand new Gucci jacket he'd gotten from New York, and grabbed the beeper. He walked across the room to the phone, and dialed his grandma's number, while taking another yawn.

"Hello?" a female voice answered.

"Ma?" Lemar asked, surprised to hear her voice.

"Lemar, I've been calling you all day. Why are you just calling me back, boy?" Loretta snapped.

"I just woke up," he replied, scratching his head. He looked at his watch. "What you doing over Grandma's house at this time of night? Is everything okay?"

Loretta sighed. "No, everything isn't okay."

"What's wrong? Is Grandma sick?"

"Your grandmother is just fine," Loretta said.

"Then why aren't you at home?"

There was a long pause. "Because it was broken into," she answered.

"Broken into?"

"Yes, broken into." Loretta sighed again. "The worst part is the police seem to think that Maurice has been abducted. They even found blood stains on my bedroom rug."

Lemar shook his head as he thought about Doug. *I can't believe that niggah would stoop so low*. Lemar closed his eyes. He put the phone down and silently cursed, as mixed emotions overcame him. "Ma, I'll find him. I promise." Lemar said, putting the phone back to his ear.

"Damn it, Lemar! What have you done?" Loretta shouted.

Young Assassin

"I can't discuss it over the phone, Ma. I'll talk to you later. It'll be okay."

He immediately hung up the phone and reached into the same pocket of his jacket for his car keys, as he hurried out the dorm to his car.

❊ ❊ ❊

As Lemar traveled down the Avenue, he gently guided the steering wheel of his Black '87 Lamborghini. His heart pounded like a drum inside his chest. He breathed heavily, as he attempted to find a way to shake off the anxiety that stuck to his mind. If anything terrible happened to Maurice, he wouldn't be able to forgive himself.

He saw a group of young'uns standing on the corner of Ninth and Kalhoun Avenue, smoking and talking shit to one another. The moment he pulled over, they all looked at him strangely, especially when he got out the car and walked over to them.

"Which one of y'all is J.B.?" he asked.

All of them looked at him with blank faces. Everyone had heard of Lemar, had seen him drive through the neighborhood constantly, and looked up to him. Now here he was -- Big Time Lemar, the King of D.C.

One of the young'uns stepped forward. "I'm J.B.," he said, snacking on a huge Snickers bar. "What's up?"

"My brother mentioned your name to me before. He said you were his boy."

J.B. grinned. "I need to find Bandit," Lemar said. "You know where he at?"

"Up on Tilden Place at the playground wit' Troy," J.B. replied.

Lemar reached in his back pocket and pulled out a miniature bankroll. He stepped to J.B., and handed him two crisp one hundred dollar bills. He turned, got back into his car, and sped off, while J.B. looked at the sporty black vehicle in astonishment.

It took Lemar less than a minute to reach the playground. He parked his prized possession and got out. The playground was made up of sliding boards, swings, and a basketball court outside a small recreation center. He walked onto the court, and saw Troy and Bandit leaning on a fence. He walked over to them in a fast pace.

"What's up fellas?" he said, without allowing them to answer. "Long story short, my little brother has been kidnapped," Lemar told them. "The niggah who did it is gonna kill him if I don't account for the money, or the coke that I was robbed of, so I really need your help, Bandit."

Troy frowned, with a bewildered look. "Maurice has been kidnapped?" he asked.

"Yeah," Lemar answered. "And time is wasting."

"I'll help too. Whatever it takes to get Maurice back, I'll do it," Troy said. "You know he's my boy. What's the dude's name who kidnapped him?"

"Doug, and he lives in Maryland, near Adelphi." Lemar looked at Bandit, who already had his gun in hand, but never said a word.

Bandit was a hot head, who was known around the hood as a cold-blooded killer. Word on the street was that he had at least forty murders under his belt. He'd even done a few jobs for Lemar in the past.

"Man, it's gonna cost you two g's up front," Bandit finally said.

Lemar continued to stare at Bandit, and wondered how he became such a threat in the first place. Bandit's short, 5'3 inch frame and extremely slim build, always reminded him of a ten year old boy. Lemar smiled as he thought, *even a feather could knock his little ass over. Maybe being ruthless makes up for his small statue.*

"So, you wanna do this or what?" Bandit asked, breaking Lemar from his trance.

"Cool," Lemar replied. "I'm gonna call Doug, and make up some shit about having his money. When we run up in his spot, I need you to shoot everything moving." He looked down at the gun in Bandit's hand. "You gonna need more than that six-shooter."

Bandit reached into his coat and retrieved a Tec-9mm. "Is this enough?" he asked, looking at Lemar with a killer expression. "Niggah, I know how to put in my work."

Lemar smiled. "I'll be right back."

He walked up the block to a pay phone, and dialed Doug's phone number. Lemar took a few deep breaths as he waited for him to answer.

"Yes?" a feminine voice answered on the third ring.

"Alvina, let me speak to Doug."

It took several minutes for Doug to answer.

"This Doug," he finally said.

"What the fuck do you call yourself doing? Having your people break in my mom's house, and kidnapping my little brother, you punk!" Lemar roared.

"You wanna mess with me, young boy?" Doug asked, getting hyped. "Cause if you do, you know where to find me."

"Fuck you!" Lemar shouted into the phone.

"Fuck me? Motherfucka, you got until five a.m. to bring me my money, or the paramedics are gonna be scraping your little brother's dead ass up off the street somewhere," Doug shot back, before slamming the phone down.

As Lemar returned to the playground, he saw Troy coming toward him.

"What's up? You screaming and yelling loud enough to wake up the whole block," Troy said. "What did he say?"

"He said he's gonna kill Maurice by five a.m. if I don't bring him the money."

"So, what you gonna do?" Troy gave him a look, that assured Lemar he was on his side. He even tried to transform his baby face into a ruthless look.

"Fuck that niggah! His bitch ass is gonna pay for messing with my little brother."

"So, let's do this!" Troy replied, pulling his baseball cap low onto his head.

At that moment, Lemar looked at Troy like a concerned parent. He knew Troy's older brother, Seth, would object to him wanting Troy to do his dirt, but Maurice's life was at stake, and he knew Doug wasn't playing. He had to do something, and fast.

"Listen, this isn't a game. Have you ever killed anybody?" Lemar inquired.

Troy shivered, from the cold air. "Man, I'm not a kid anymore. I know I look like the baby of the crew, but I know how to put in work too. I just need some steel. You got one I can use?" he asked.

"Yeah," Lemar answered. "But first I need to switch cars. Wait here for me, I'll be back to get y'all."

"Okay," Troy said. "How far is your other ride?"

"Just a five minute drive, near the Ibex Club. I'll be right back." Lemar hurried to his vehicle and gunned the engine. After quickly pulling out the parking space, the Lamborghini zoomed down the street.

❊　❊　❊

Sebastian sat on the living room floor of Doug's condominium, with two 9mms by his side, as he prepared to perform a heartless murder. The thought of murdering a kid didn't bother him at all. As long as the money was right, Sebastian could care less. He anticipated the gory scene he'd be creating in just a few hours. He looked at his watch, waiting for the go-ahead from Doug. It was a little past midnight. He went over to the sofa, to where the kilo Doug had given him rested on the cushions. Sebastian picked it up, took it into the kitchen, and got a spoon from the sink full of dishes.

He wiped the dirty spoon on his clothes, and opened the plastic that was wrapped around the coke. Sebastian dipped the spoon in the coke, snorted a teaspoon full, and wiped off what remained on his nose. He took the remaining coke and placed it in a cabinet above the stove, and tossed the spoon back into the sink.

"That's some good shit," he said, playing with his nose.

Sebastian went back into the living room, and stood at the window, looking down at the busy traffic along the Prince George's County freeway.

In the bedroom, Doug and Alvina laid in the bed, both disgusted with one another. Doug wanted sex, but Alvina refused and pushed him away several times. *How could he hit me*? she thought continuously.

Doug moved his body on top of her and sucked on her neck, but she pushed him away again. "What the fuck is your problem?" he asked, turning on the light.

"You," she said. "Did you forget that you smacked me earlier, and now you expect me to have sex with you!"

"Of course I do. I smack your ass around all the time, and it's never stopped us from fucking before." Doug looked at Alvina's perfect body in the sexy black lace nightgown she wore. "Look, I'm sorry about what happened earlier," he said, rubbing her arm.

"Like hell you are!" Alvina screamed, looking at him.

Doug smiled. "I know what's really bothering you. You're thinking about that kid aren't you?"

"Yeah, I'm thinking about him, but I'm still pissed off with you for disrespecting me."

"Well, don't worry about him, because he's gonna die regardless."

"Is he really? You know, I heard you arguing with Lemar over the phone earlier, and do you know what I think?"

"What?" Doug asked uninterested.

"I think Lemar is gonna run up in this place with a whole bunch of guys and kill your ass, and I don't want to be caught in the crossfire." She jumped out of the bed and walked to the closet.

"Lemar knows better. Besides, he doesn't have the balls to do something like that. He's a pretty boy, you know…doesn't like to get his hands dirty," Doug responded.

"If his little brother's life is at stake, his balls can be larger than life." She reached into the closet and grabbed a black sweater and a pair of jeans.

"Where do you think you're goin'?" he asked.

Alvina ignored his question. "I can't believe I got engaged to someone as cruel as you. I can see you killing a guy if he owes you money, but I can't understand why a young kid who doesn't owe you anything has to suffer."

She quickly slipped out of her nightgown, and into her clothes. After picking up her purse, she reached in the closet to get her brown leather trench coat and python-skin boots, before walking out the room.

Doug followed her, with satin sheets covering his body. "Now isn't the time to play fucking games with me!" he shouted. "Where are you goin'?"

Alvina walked into the living room, and saw Sebastian on the sofa with two guns on his lap. They stared at each other for a few seconds, before Doug grabbed her arm.

"I'm gonna ask you one more fucking time. Where are you

goin'?" he repeated. Doug was growing tired of asking the same question, without receiving a valid answer.

"I'm going to take the boy some food like I promised him," she said. "I'll be back in an hour." She looked at him, and swallowed as he let go of her arm.

❉   ❉   ❉

Troy and Bandit rode in the backseat of Lemar's Cabriolet as he sped past the Maryland state line. Only two things mattered to Lemar at the moment -- to get Maurice, and to kill Doug.

He entered a suburban neighborhood with beautiful houses, and perfectly smooth streets. Lemar immediately spotted the condominium where Doug lived in full view as he looked ahead.

"We're almost there," he said.

"Good," Troy responded, holding Lemar's sawed-off shotgun and 9mm in his lap, anticipating murder.

Lemar slowed the car down as they approached the parking lot of Doug's house. As they went over a speed bump, they watched a red Corvette speed by. Lemar thought he saw Alvina behind the wheel, but wasn't sure.

"I'm gonna call Doug, and tell him to meet me outside." Lemar pulled out a black cellular bag phone from the backseat.

"I hope that's not your phone, because when we pop this niggah, that shit could come back on you," Bandit said.

"No, one of my crackheads stole it for me," Lemar responded. "Look, you two get out and hide behind a car, and as soon as he comes out, I want y'all to blast his ass," Lemar ordered.

"But what if he insists that you come up there?" Bandit asked.

"Good question." Lemar thought hard for a few seconds. "Well, then give me about a minute to settle in, and then y'all come up, shoot down the door and start tearing up everything in sight."

Whatever way it went down, Lemar felt the whole thing could've been avoided if only Doug had reasoned with him. But since he didn't, it had come down to this.

Lemar dialed Doug's number, and waited for someone to pick up.

"Hello?" Doug said.

"I got your money," Lemar responded. "Do you want me to come up, because I'm outside of your crib."

"I knew you would come around, Lemar, my boy," Doug said. "No, meet me in the parking lot of the Maryland Community Library on Westernburgh Pike in forty minutes."

"I'll be there," Lemar said. He hung up the phone and looked at Troy and Bandit. "Change of plans." He backed the car up and skidded out the parking lot.

Young Assassin

Chapter Three

Maurice shivered in the darkness, as he yearned for comfort and warmth. He began to feel a disturbing pain inside his chest, as he breathed in the cold air through his nostrils. His eyes were shut tight as tears slid down his face. His fingers were so cold he could barely move them. Mucus dripped from his nostrils. The slight headache he'd had earlier had turned into an agonizing migraine, and his back ached because of his awkward position.

This has to be a bad dream, he thought. *This can't be happenin'.*

Maurice heard the sound of footsteps coming. It was the same sound he'd heard hours ago, except the steps seemed to be quicker. Suddenly, he heard a clicking sound, and once again, light beamed from above, blinding him for the second time. He looked toward the door, and through blurred vision, saw the same short figure approaching him. Maurice started to cry again, as he felt the tender touch of a soothing hand on his shoulder. Then to his surprise, the cloth was removed from his mouth.

"Are you okay?" she asked.

"It's you," he said, as he coughed up deep congestion. He spit over his shoulder, and looked up at her.

"Yes, it's me, Alvina." She untied him as fast as she could. "I've got to get you out of here. If your brother doesn't pay Doug by five o'clock, he's gonna have you killed."

Maurice looked at her. "Why are you doing this? How do I know you're not tricking me?"

"Trust me," Alvina said to him. "I just can't stand by and see an innocent kid like you die." She snatched the rope from around his ankles and looked at him. "Can you stand up?"

"I think so," Maurice responded.

Even if Alvina was lying to him, he had nowhere else to turn. His best bet was to go along with her. He felt stiff as he struggled to his feet. He stretched, and took three steps toward the door. Alvina took off her coat and wrapped it around his body.

"Come on," she said. "I have to get you to the car, and into some heat."

She knew Doug would kill her if he ever found out what she had just done. Alvina guided Maurice out the door as he shivered in the severe cold on their way to her car. She helped him into the passenger side, and slammed the door.

Alvina rubbed her arms, as a cold gust of wind settled on her body. She quickly got into the car and pulled off like a race car driver. As they rode in silence, she looked over at Maurice, who stared out the window with a blank expression. *He may never get over this,* she thought.

A few moments later, her thoughts turned to Doug. Alvina knew that after he found out what she'd done, their relationship would be over. But in her heart what she'd done was the right thing. She reached over and placed her hand on Maurice's forehead.

"You have a fever," she said. "I'm so sorry this had to happen."

Maurice never turned his head.

❉ ❉ ❉

Ten lampposts stood overhead, beaming down on the parking lot of the Maryland Community Library, as Lemar stood by his car with a briefcase in his hand, waiting for Doug to arrive. He looked up at the two flagpoles that stood tall, and flapped wildly in the wind. He sighed into the frigid air, wishing Doug would hurry up so this whole thing could be over.

Lemar looked to his left, toward Westernburgh Pike, and spotted what appeared to be headlights approaching from a hundred yards away. Suddenly, he saw the left turn signal flashing, as the car came closer. *This has to be Doug,* Lemar thought.

At that moment his pager beeped. He ignored it as a four-door, money-green Jaguar XJ6 entered the parking lot. Lemar took a deep breath, feeling the anxiety building back up again.

The car stopped across from Lemar's vehicle. A rear window rolled down, and Doug's face appeared from the darkness. "You got my money, young boy?" Doug asked.

Lemar lifted the briefcase. "It's right here."

"Well, bring it over here," Doug replied.

"No. Send somebody to come get it, or come get it yourself," Lemar stated his demand as calmly as he could. "And tell me where my little brother is."

There was a long silence, while some conversation appeared to be going on inside the automobile. A few moments later, Doug, stepped out.

He had on a long fur coat, a skull cap and a pair of Timberland boots. Two other men also got out, and followed Doug to where Lemar stood. Lemar looked at them, as a lump formed in his throat.

"Sebastian, take the briefcase and open it up," Doug commanded.

Sebastian walked over to Lemar and snatched the briefcase from his hand. He looked into Lemar's eyes very sternly, and turned the briefcase right side up. His gaze shifted to the briefcase as he opened it.

"This is bullshit! It's full of motherfuckin' confetti!" Sebastian yelled.

"It's a fucking setup!" Doug screamed.

Instantly, the sounds of gunshots rang out. Lemar took cover as Sebastian reached for both of his 9mms and started shooting in all directions. Sebastian turned around and saw two figures charging at them with firearms pointing. Before he could defend himself, he took a huge bullet from a shotgun directly in the stomach, the slug ripping his mid-section wide open. He fell face forward onto the concrete, spitting up blood in the process.

"I'm gonna kill your fucking brother!" Doug screamed. He ran back to the car and tried to get inside, but three shots hit his arm, as another one hit him on the side of his face. He dropped to his knees and fell on his side. He slowly tried to get up, but was hit with even more bullets.

Shots rang out all over, leaving Doug's entourage lifeless. Doug tried again to push himself up off the ground, as six more bullets hit him in the spine. A shotgun blast then sounded, the slug pounding him in the upper back. Then the gunfire ceased.

"Let's roll!" Lemar shouted.

He ran toward his car and got inside. Troy and Bandit got into the backseat as Lemar put the car in gear and sped away.

Lemar entered Uptown fifteen minutes later. He drove down the street, feeling high and mighty, as well as regretful. He was truly sorry that Doug had to die, especially since he still didn't know about Maurice's whereabouts.

Lemar reached into his jacket for his pager. He'd almost forgotten about the page he'd gotten earlier, just before the fireworks. He looked at the screen and frowned at the unfamiliar number. Normally he wouldn't even consider calling the number back, but he had to make an exception this time. *Maybe someone has information about Maurice,* Lemar thought, as he pulled out the stolen cell phone and dialed the number.

"Hello."

"Who's this?" Lemar asked.

"Lemar, it's Alvina. I just wanted you to know that I saved your brother a little while ago. He's in the Intensive Care Unit at Howard University Hospital."

A sense of relief instantly filled Lemar's body. He was glad his little brother was alive. "Intensive Care Unit? What's wrong with him?" He figured Maurice had given her his pager number.

"He has a fever of a hundred and five degrees, and the doctors said that he has pneumonia," she replied. "Doug was about to do something terrible to him, but I couldn't allow that to happen. So I took it upon myself to get him out of there."

"Thank you, Alvina," he said.

There was a pause. Lemar knew the question was coming. He braced himself.

"How did your meeting with Doug go?" she asked.

"A lot less than peaceful, I'm afraid."

"Is he...?"

"Yeah, he is," Lemar responded, before Alvina could finish. "I didn't want it to come to that. I tried to talk to Doug when that robbery went down, but he wasn't trying to listen. He really fucked up when he kidnapped Maurice, so unfortunately this was the outcome. I'm sorry."

"Are you coming to see your brother?" she asked in a low voice, appearing to be untouched by the information of Doug's fate.

"No, I'm not," he said. "I have to turn myself in to D.C.P.D. right away."

"For what?"

Lemar smiled. "Because I have a warrant out for my arrest." He looked up into the dark sky, as he stopped at a light. "Alvina, I gotta go. I hope you're not mad at me."

"I'm not mad at you, Lemar. Actually, I don't know how to feel at this point."

In a strange way, Lemar felt that she had gained his trust. "I need to get in contact with my mother. Please stay with my brother until she gets there. And thank you again."

"You're welcome," she said, hanging up the phone.

Lemar's smile was even wider as he thought about his brother. "Maurice is alive," he said.

"Are you serious, niggah? How do you know?" Troy asked.

"I just talked to Doug's girl, Alvina. She took Maurice to the hospital."

"Damn, that's a fucking relief," Bandit responded. "But she's probably gonna freak out once she finds out we just killed that niggah, Doug."

Lemar didn't respond. He couldn't figure out why Alvina wasn't mad. Bandit and Troy sat quietly in the backseat as Lemar took them back to the playground on Tilden Place.

"I'll holla at y'all later!" Lemar yelled out the window, as Bandit and Troy got out.

"Tell my niggah, Maurice, I said what's up!" Troy yelled back.

Within minutes, Lemar was back in his dorm room. He quickly changed into a Sergio Techni sweatsuit and a pair of Adidas tennis shoes, and put his old clothes and shoes into a trash bag. He had to get rid of any evidence that could place him at the scene of the crime. Before he headed out, he took one last look around his room. *Hopefully, it won't be long before I come back,* he thought, as he locked the door.

He walked up several blocks before finding a dumpster behind a building, and tossed the bag along with crushed pieces of the cell phone inside. Lemar walked in the cold air until he spotted a cab. He waved the yellow car down, and asked the driver to take him to the Fourth District Precinct.

When Lemar got out the cab, he walked to a pay phone diagonally across the street, outside a huge church, and dialed his grandmother's number.

"Hello?" Loretta said.

"Ma, you still up?"

"Yes, I'm still up. Did you find Maurice? Is he safe? Is he alive?" she said, all in one breath.

"Ma, Maurice is fine. He's at Howard University Hospital. He's being treated for pneumonia. I would've gone to visit him, but..."

Loretta quickly hung up the phone. Lemar nodded, knowing his mother was on her way to the hospital to be near her son. As he stood holding the phone, he looked across the street toward the two-story, tan brick police station. After gently placing the phone back on the receiver, he walked in the direction of the precinct and went inside.

He stood in the lobby, looking at the soda machine. He turned left, and saw two police officers staring at him from behind a large counter. Lemar walked over and took a deep breath.

"Sir, can we help you with something?" one of the cops asked.

"My name is Lemar Patterson," he said to them, as his heart raced. "I'm wanted on drug charges and I'm turning myself in."

Young Assassin

Chapter Four

The sun blazed over Washington, D.C. on a hot and humid summer afternoon in June. The temperature was a scorching ninety-three degrees, as Maurice and Tia walked slowly down Kalhoun Avenue, holding hands.

Tia was six months pregnant, with a baby boy due in a few months. Although the baby wasn't his, Maurice was excited about it. The baby's real father was a well-known local college basketball star headed for the NBA.

With his seventeenth birthday having just passed, Maurice was slowly starting to change. Despite his mother's disapproval, he'd gone out and gotten two large tattoos on his left shoulder. He wasn't the skinny, naïve Maurice his family and friends were used too. Although he'd always managed to hang out with his crew, he still maintained his innocence; but he was starting to feel like he needed to prove himself to the world, especially to the streets of D.C.

All his friends were involved in criminal activities, and his brother was one of the biggest drug-dealers around town. Maurice had promised his mother that he'd never go that route, but now he was considering it.

He never thought the peer pressure would get to him, and that he'd desire a life a crime; but for some reason, his mind kept drifting back to the night he was kidnapped. Although he hated what Doug and Sebastian did to him, he admired their style. Putting fear into the hearts of men, just like Sebastian did to him, was all he could think about. Gangsta, was what he called it, and he wanted to one day be just like them.

As usual, the Avenue was pumping, drugs were being bought

and sold non-stop. Maurice and Tia stopped on Eighth and Kalhoun, and stared deep into each other's eyes. To Tia, Maurice seemed to be preoccupied lately. She wondered if anything was going on in his life that she didn't know about, and if there was, of course she wanted him to let her in on it.

They reached Oak Terrace a few minutes later. Maurice studied the drug dealers, who wore huge gold around their necks, as they sold their supply to dirty, disgusting looking crackheads. Men and women had who bodies that appeared to have had the life sucked out of them.

Maurice followed Tia up the four-step staircase to her apartment. The elevator was always broken. She unlocked the door and let him in, before stepping inside and quietly shutting the door. Suddenly, a young man rushed into the living room, with a pistol in his hand, and gazed at them with an evil look. He was fair-skinned, with a 6'4 frame, which towered over Maurice. He wore an Atlanta Hawks jersey, long red shorts, and had a killer-like instinct.

"Brian," Tia called out, "Why you runnin' to the door like dat? It's just me and Maurice. You scared somebody gonna run up in here?"

Brian was Tia's annoying older brother, who had met Maurice a few years ago, when he'd taken Tia to their junior high school prom. For some reason, Brian really liked Maurice's style. Maurice was quiet, yet tough, which was rare in the hood. "What's up?" he said to Maurice, a smile spreading across his face.

"What's up?" Maurice replied. He looked at the pistol. "You can put that thing away now."

"I just needed to make sure y'all wasn't tryin' to rob a nig-gah," Brian replied, as he put the pistol under the cushions of the sofa.

Maurice looked around. Things had changed since the last

time he'd been there. A large color television stood against the wall, and a Nintendo entertainment game system rested on the floor. *Damn, they getting money around here,* Maurice thought.

"Brian, what's been up?" Maurice asked, as he and Tia sat on the sofa.

"I been doin' what a lot of folks in America been doin'," he said.

"What's that?" Maurice asked.

"Steady hustling. You ain't tried to hustle yet?"

Maurice looked at him for a second before answering. "Nah, man."

"Lemar's got a good grip on you, huh?" Brian asked, with a huge grin.

"Lemar ain't got nothing on me," Maurice responded defensively.

"Whatever," Brian said laughing. "You know good and well dat Lemar would kick yo ass if he caught you out on the Avenue sellin' rocks."

"It ain't even like that. I just don't want to put my freedom in jeopardy," he explained. Maurice was generally a quiet, low key kind of guy, but he made it his business to show that he was his own man.

Brian really cracked up that time. "You mean to tell me dat you never thought about being a hustler before?"

"Yeah, I've thought about it," Maurice replied.

"Well, why haven't you tried it?"

"Because my brother gives me everything I need," Maurice said. "I couldn't be happier with what I already have."

"Must be nice," Brian said sarcastically.

"Boy, leave him alone!" Tia ordered.

"I'm just tryin' to see where he at." He gave Maurice a slap on the back. "I know you look up to Lemar, but you ain't no lil kid no more. You gotta be your own man now. What would you do if

Lemar dropped dead today or tomorrow? Then who would you have to look up to? Yourself, right?"

Maurice glanced at Tia, who gave him a supportive look.

"Maurice, don't worry about him," Tia said. "Or for dat matter, nothin' his dumb ass says."

"Yeah, don't worry 'bout me," Brian said, walking out the room.

Maurice instantly began to think about his crew. J.B. was into drugs, and dabbled into anything illegal that Troy brought his way. Troy and Bandit enjoyed robbing a few people here and there, and even wiped out a major drug-dealer, who had a solid reputation for being a brutal killer. Maurice shook his head as his thoughts continued. He was obviously troubled by something -- something that kept him searching for an answer.

"Are you okay?" Tia asked, reaching for his hand.

"Maybe. Yeah. I don't know," Maurice said, with a bit of uncertainty in his reply.

Tia began to rub his arm. "Lately you've been into yourself. Even when we're together you're quiet, it's like you're anti-social or somethin'. Is everything okay?"

"It ain't nothing like that," he answered.

"Then, what is it?"

"Well, for one, I miss Lemar since my mother put him out a few years ago," Maurice said. "I see him every now and then, but it's not the same."

"Is that all?" Tia asked.

"No, lately I've been feeling the urge to do the wrong thing."

"You're not alone. We all face dat in our lives at sometime or another."

"I don't think we're talking about the same thing Tia," Maurice responded, with frustration.

"I'm confused."

Maurice sighed. "I wanna be like my brother. You know with

his fly cars and major paper."

"But your brother is a big-time drug-dealer," she responded. "It would take you a few years, or perhaps even more, to get on the level dat he's at. Doesn't he look after you and give you everything you want?"

"Yeah, but it's like I'm being controlled by him somehow. He gives me money, but he doesn't give me the material things I want."

"Like what?" she asked.

He looked at her and smiled. "Like a BMW or a 300ZX."

Tia sucked her teeth and shook her head.

"Seriously, Brian's right. I'm not a little child anymore. There's gonna come a time, sooner or later, when I'm gonna have to take care of myself."

"But it doesn't have to be now, Maurice. You have your whole life ahead of you. If you give into temptation, you'll be transformed and will never be the same again."

"I've tried whatever I could do to resist the temptation, but I've found it totally pointless."

"What about your mother? If she ever finds out dat you're a hustler, it'll break her heart."

"I know," he replied. "But even if it's just to sell weed, I wanna experience that other side of life."

Tia put her arm around him. She finally understood what he was going through. Maurice wanted material things, but he didn't have the means to get them. *Maybe sellin' drugs is not such a bad thing,* Tia thought. *Everybody does it.*

"I'm about to walk back around my way," he said, standing up to leave.

She walked him to the door and kissed him on the cheek. "Be careful on your way out of here."

Maurice smiled. "I will."

❋ ❋ ❋

Kalhoun Avenue was becoming more and more known throughout D.C. Located at the very top of Uptown, just below Shepherd Park, the place was always busy with crime. It if wasn't drug smuggling, it was prostitution, and if it wasn't that, then it was someone being shot dead or seriously wounded in the street.

As J.B. and Troy walked up one of the residential blocks along the Avenue, they caught glimpses of crackheads walking around in a daze, and flashy automobiles going up and down the street.

"Man, I can't wait to get me a fly ass car," J.B. said, as a new Audi drove past.

"Yeah I know. I can't get any pussy walking like this," Troy replied.

Both of them had been hustling for a while, but still hadn't managed to make any real money. J.B. was about to graduate from high school, while Troy had dropped out a few months ago. Troy had a hard life growing up around Omorafe Manor, one of the roughest neighborhoods in D.C., and it had a negative effect on his life at a young age.

They stopped outside a twenty-four hour store on the corner of Sixth and Kalhoun, a block away from Troy's house. The store had been there for years, and had become a hangout spot for all the local hustlers. The owners even sold minors alcohol for the right price. J.B. stood outside, while Troy went in to get a beer. By the time Troy came out, J.B. had served three crackheads.

"You ain't bring me nothing?" J.B. said, as they walked up the Avenue. "A Baby Ruth, Kit Kat...somethin'."

"Man, your ass is fat enough," Troy said, opening the beer. He put the bottle to his mouth and took a few sips. "Want some?"

"Nah, I'm cool," J.B. responded. He knew he needed to lose

some weight "What's up wit' Bandit? I haven't heard from him."

"He went to get some arms, so we can make our move later on."

"What move?" J.B. asked.

"Me and Bandit gonna rob a bank right before it closes today," Troy responded, taking a few more sips.

J.B. smiled as he looked at Troy. "Which bank y'all gonna hit?"

"American National," he said. "You wanna join us?"

"Hell yeah. You know I'm down for that type of shit."

"Cool. Then all we have to do is wait for Bandit to come back wit' the steel."

From the way Troy spoke, J.B. knew this was serious, and wondered if he'd robbed a bank before.

"Is this y'all first bank robbery?" J.B. asked.

"Yeah. We didn't get enough money when we robbed Fat Ronald on McDuffie Street a few months ago, so we decided to go for something bigger."

"Damn! Why didn't y'all tell me about that?"

"It was some spare of the moment type shit," Troy replied. He took a few more swallows of his beer. "Man, those fools from McDuffie Street are cut throats, but I'm gonna rob his fat ass again."

"You better let me get down with that shit," J.B. said.

As Troy laughed at his friend, he caught a glimpse of a familiar person walking in their direction.

"What's up, Maurice?" Troy said.

"What's up?" Maurice responded, as he came in contact with his friends. He shook Troy's free hand, and slapped J.B. on his back.

"Where you coming from?" Troy asked.

He and Maurice had become like brothers over the last few years. They both had attended Coolidge High School together, until Troy dropped out to sell drugs full time.

"Oak Terrace," Maurice replied, "Visiting my girl."

J.B. and Troy had heard about the drug infested Oak Terrace. All the youngsters who lived around that neighborhood sold drugs, and were violent crews of thieves, cut throats, and murderers.

The trio walked up the block in the miserable humidity. As sweat poured downed his face, J.B. decided to take his friend up on the offer.

"On second thought, gimme some beer." Troy smiled. He handed J.B. the bottle, as he guzzled down what was left.

"Where we on our way to?" Maurice asked.

"Let's go to our spot," J.B. said, dropping the empty bottle on the sidewalk.

Once they reached the playground, they saw two police officers standing on the basketball court, and about twelve to fifteen guys standing with their hands in the air as they were being searched.

"That's Officer Bailey and his partner," Troy said pointing. "His fat ass is the one who came and locked up my brother after he got set up." He turned to look at J.B. "If you got any rocks on you, I suggest you start walkin' in the other direction, 'cause these motherfuckin' cops are petty as shit."

At that moment, Officer Bailey looked in their direction, but didn't seem to pay them any mind.

"Officer Reynolds," they heard Bailey say to the other policeman. "Keep your gun pointed at these punks." He looked at all the guys one by one. "I'm gonna search and frisk you. Give me any problems, and your ass is gonna get popped!"

"Listen to that fool," Troy said. "D.C.P.D. has three thousand cops, and twenty-five hundred of them are cruddy as a motherfucka!"

Bailey frisked every guy on the court, and they all came up clean.

"Shit," he said, apparently disappointed that he didn't find anything. He turned his back and looked up at the sky. His protruding belly hung over his tightly fitted uniform pants, and always caused everyone to make fun of his appearance.

"Your fat ass is so fucking petty," one of the young men said. "Slob," he ended.

Bailey immediately turned around. "Who said that?" he questioned, reaching for his club.

"I said it," a tall, dark guy said, walking up in Bailey's face.

Bailey looked at the guy with a smile. Then his demeanor changed, as he swung the club upside the guy's head, and beat him mercilessly.

Officer Reynolds rushed over to restrain his partner. Luckily, he was much taller and stronger than Bailey. He grabbed the club from Bailey's hand and tossed it to the ground.

"Get off me!" Bailey growled.

Reynolds let go, as Bailey picked the club up off the ground. He looked at the guys on the basketball court. "All you scum better lay low!" he yelled, pointing his club at them for emphasis. His gaze shifted to the guy he'd beaten, lying unconscious on the ground. "Use his ass as an example not to fuck with me!" Bailey said, as he and his partner walked away.

Both men walked by J.B., Maurice and Troy, and hurried off.

"Somebody's gonna kill that fool," Troy said, watching the two officers get into their squad car.

Maurice walked to where the fallen guy was and knelt before him, while Troy stared at the squad car as it turned off Tilden Place.

"I hate that niggah," J.B. said.

Young Assassin

The apartment was empty, except for a bed and small television located in the bedroom. Alvina's pants rested near her ankles, as she held on to the edge of the bed. Lemar looked at Alvina's shapely round ass and proudly took his position behind her. He was more than ready to enter her treasure, and loving every bit of their powerful foreplay. The summer heat had made their erotic encounter even more pleasurable, as perspiration dampened their partially naked bodies.

The smell of sex began to dominate the room as Lemar pounded Alvina from behind. With every stroke, her moans grew louder. She shook her head wildly, and shut her eyes, as the feeling of pleasure consumed her small body. Within minutes, they both were having orgasms that could be heard a block away.

Lemar smacked her ass. "Was Doug ever that good?"

"Not even close," she admitted, wondering why he'd bring up her ex-fiancé's name after such a special moment.

Alvina smiled, as she thought about the first time she saw Lemar with Doug. She'd been infatuated with him ever since. She always felt they made the perfect match, and sometimes even imagined them having a child together. Most of all, she'd always been mesmerized by Lemar's good looks. His smooth light-brown skin and beautiful green eyes had every girl crazy about him. They were especially attracted to his deep pockets, but that didn't phase Alvina.

She was the first girl, who didn't press him for money. She loved Lemar for who he was, and not for what he had. And although Lemar was Alvina's third boyfriend from the game, he treated her better than anyone else. He never raised his hand, or even his voice like Doug.

After the ordeal with Maurice's abduction, over two years ago, Alvina and Maurice hung out periodically. She even went with him to visit Lemar, while he was serving his sentence on drug possession charges. Other hustlers on the outside wanted

40

her, but she found herself becoming emotionally involved with Lemar. When she started receiving collect calls from Lemar on a regular basis, she started feeling something that went beyond friendship. Once he got out of jail, their relationship blossomed.

"I'm about to take a shower," Lemar said, "You coming?"

Alvina smiled. "Go ahead and run the water. I'll be there in a minute."

An hour later, Lemar and Alvina left their new apartment in the suburbs of Germantown, Maryland, and headed straight for D.C.

Lemar cruised in his new cherry red Mercedes 190E down the freeway, with Alvina holding his hand while they listened to the radio. He'd recently put his Lamborghini in storage and purchased the Benz a few days after his release. Lemar was dressed in a red Gucci sweatsuit, and a white Madness hat with assorted letters that represented Uptown.

Alvina closed her eyes as Lemar grabbed her hand, and held it gently. Suddenly, a smile appeared once she felt the warmth of his mouth, as Lemar sucked each of her fingers.

"Boy, you are so nasty," Alvina said, with a wide grin.

Young Assassin

Chapter Five

Tia got up off the sofa and strutted to her room. A few minutes later, she came back with her keys in hand, and walked toward the front door of the apartment.

"Where you goin'?" Tia's mother, Bonita asked.

"I'm goin' to see Craig. We need to talk about child support."

"At this time of night? It's almost eleven-thirty."

"I know, but I wanna talk to him face-to-face."

Bonita shook her head. "I can't believe it took you so long to talk to him. How are you gettin' there?"

"My cab should already be downstairs," Tia responded.

"Well, why can't his ass come and get you?" Bonita questioned. "Maybe you should ask Maurice to go with you."

"Ma, I'll be fine. Don't worry," Tia said, as she opened the door and left.

She made it downtown a half an hour later. Tia paid the cabbie and walked down Ninth Street to Craig's apartment. His block consisted of townhouses on both sides of the street, with the exception of a small efficiency apartment building that sat on the corner. She hadn't seen Craig since they'd broken up over four months ago. Even though she disliked the notion of it, she still had a special place in her heart for him. He had been her first love, and the guy to whom she'd lost her virginity.

Her mother's words of advice concerning her child burned within her mind, as she opened the door to the apartment building. She walked down the familiar narrow hallway that led to an elevator. When Tia got off, she walked to Apartment #606 and knocked.

Young Assassin

A tall, brown-skinned young man standing 6'9', who wore torn blue jeans and no shirt, answered the door, and looked at Tia strangely.

"Long time, no see," he said, allowing her to come in. "Is this visit business or pleasure?"

"I'm not in the mood for nonsense, Craig," she responded.

The strong odor of weed and sex instantly burned her nose, as she walked into the apartment. Tia shook her head at the small unclean space. She looked at the dusty blue sleeping bag on the floor, and the small bag of white powder lying next to it.

"Are you selling drugs now?" Tia asked, pointing to the coke.

"Nah, that shit is for me. I get high sometimes," Craig replied. "Do you want some?"

"Hell, no!" she shouted. "Did you forget dat I'm pregnant?"

Tia looked at Craig as he picked up the bag of coke. He reached into his back pocket, and pulled out a five-dollar bill and rolled it. He then opened the bag, stuffed the rolled bill into it, put it to his right nostril, and snorted.

"I can't believe you're doin' drugs now," Tia said, with a disgusted stare.

He smiled and clapped his hands. "Why did you come here? Oh, you probably came to make up, right?" Craig began pulling his pants down.

"Listen, I came to talk to you about our baby," Tia responded, pointing to her stomach.

"What about your baby?"

"Our baby! And I came to tell you that I expect your ass to pay child support."

Craig laughed as he pulled his underwear off. He threw them on the bed, giving Tia a full view of his naked body. "Let's you and I make another baby right now!"

"Craig, are you tripping? Besides, I have a boyfriend." Tia stood with her hands on her hips. "Are you gonna pay child support, or do I have to take you to court?"

Instantly, the smile faded from Craig's face. He walked over to her slowly. She looked at him with a serious facial expression, as he kissed her on the cheek and licked her face.

"Stop! Didn't you hear me say, I have a boyfriend?" she shouted.

"I don't care," he said. "You know you want us to get down like we used to."

Tia had enough of him. Losing her temper, as well as demanding respect, she raised her hand and slapped Craig's face so hard, that the impact sent his saliva flying across the apartment.

Craig rubbed his cheek and smiled at her. Then he swung a left hook that hit her dead in the mouth. Tia fell to her knees. Craig went to kick her in the stomach, but missed, and ended up kicking her right thigh.

"Get yo ass out my place, bitch! Hurry up!"

It took Tia a minute to get up off the floor. Carrying a five-pound load in her stomach didn't help matters. When she got to her feet, she saw him holding the door open. She cried and looked at him with tears in her eyes. He fondled her ass as she exited the apartment, then laughed and slammed the door.

❊   ❊   ❊

After Maurice returned from eating dinner with his mother, he walked to Tia's apartment. He and Brian were sitting on the living room floor playing Tecmo Bowl when Tia returned. They immediately jumped up when they saw her limping.

"What happened?" Maurice asked.

She held on to him as tightly as she could.

"What the fuck happened, Tia?" Brian asked, instantly noticing her swollen upper lip and the dried blood stuck to the outside of her mouth.

"Nothin'," she replied, resting her chin on Maurice's shoulder.

Brian frowned. "Nothin? Who did this to you?" he questioned, becoming angry.

Maurice sighed. He looked into her eyes. "Who hit you, Tia?"

Tia cupped Maurice's face, noticing more hair growing on his smooth honey colored skin. She'd always been attracted to his hairy features.

"I can't tell you," she said, looking down toward the floor.

"Forget it then," Brian said, annoyed by her answer. He walked back over and reset the game.

Maurice put both of his thumbs under her eyes and rubbed her tears away. "Why can't you tell us who did this to you?"

"Because," she said, "Brian's gonna do somethin' dumb."

"Who hit you, Tia?" Maurice asked again, losing his patience.

"Is it somebody I know?" Brian asked, from across the room.

"Yeah," Tia said, finally confessing. "It was Craig."

Brian's face became flushed. He had played street ball with Craig on numerous occasions, and thought the guy was pretty cool, but now he had fucked up. As far as Brian was concerned, Craig wasn't gonna make it to the NBA, he would see to that. He had made the biggest mistake of his life by abusing his little sister. There would be no multi-million dollar contract, no more recognition, and no more slam dunks, for his ass.

"He's gotta go," Maurice said. "And I'm not talking about to the damn NBA."

"Exactly," Brian roared with a scowl, although he was a bit surprised by Maurice's comments. He studied Maurice for a moment, as he stood in front of Tia, offering her comfort. "Damn, slim, I didn't think you were built like that. Are you really serious about killing this niggah? "

"I'm very serious," Maurice responded, with a look that sent chills through Tia.

She looked into Maurice's eyes, and saw something that frightened her. "No, Maurice, violence isn't gonna solve anything."

"The hell if it won't," Brian added.

Suddenly, Bonita came in the room. "What's goin' on?" Her face frowned as she noticed her daughter's face. "What happened, Tia?"

"Craig hit me," Tia said, running into her mother's arms.

"He still live in dat apartment downtown?" Brian asked.

Tia nodded reluctantly, as she cried on her mother's shoulder. She hated Craig for what he'd done, but she didn't want Brian or Maurice to kill him.

"How did this happen?" Maurice questioned, as he walked toward the door.

"I went to his apartment to talk to him about child support, since we've never discussed it. But when I got there, he was snorting coke, and kept talking about how he wanted to have sex with me. I ended up smacking him, and that's when he punched me." She took a deep breath. "Then he threw me out."

Maurice looked back at Brian. "Meet me on the Avenue in about an hour." He turned around and walked out the door.

"Brian, please don't do anything stupid. It's not worth it," Tia pleaded.

Brian became frustrated. "What, do you still love dat tall, sorry basketball-playin' niggah?"

"No," Tia said. "It's just wrong for you to retaliate."

"It was wrong for him to hit you."

"Two wrongs don't make it right," she persisted.

Brian smirked. "But it damn sure makes it even."

Young Assassin

❋ ❋ ❋

Troy and J.B. stood outside J.B.'s house on Milburn Street, smoking a fat blunt. J.B. blew smoke into the air, as he gazed up at the stars in the night sky. Milburn Street was the perfect spot to get blasted.

J.B. wasn't nearly the fool Troy was. He sold drugs like every other kid in the neighborhood, but he was a calmer version of Troy. J.B. had his sights set on becoming a big-time drug-dealer like Lemar. He, like all of his friends, found material possessions to be very meaningful.

J.B. looked down the street and saw a dark figure quickly approaching. Troy followed J.B.'s gaze, and as the figure got closer, he reached for his gun.

"J.B.!" a familiar voiced called out

When he finally saw the figure under the light, he smiled. "What's up, Maurice?" J.B. asked.

"I gotta go handle somebody," Maurice said.

"Who are you talking about?" J.B. asked confused.

"This dude who hit my girl, man. I'm gonna kill his ass."

"Maurice, you ain't killing nobody," J.B. said laughing. "Shut up, and let's go get something to eat."

Maurice looked at him for a second, then at Troy. "No, I'm serious. I'm about to meet my partner on the Avenue, so we can roll around the dude's way, and light his ass up." Maurice rubbed his fresh fade, wondering if they really believed him.

J.B. had never heard Maurice talk like that before. He was still trying to figure out what had possessed him to get tattoos.

Maurice looked at Troy. "If it was your girl, what would you do?"

"I'd lay that niggah down," Troy responded. "But I know you ain't gonna do nothin' like that."

"Look, Maurice," J.B. said, sounding earnest. "If you go shoot up a dude behind a girl, you could get locked up. He's gonna be dead, and in the long run, she'll probably end of with somebody else. Do you see what I'm sayin'?"

"I see what you saying, but I gotta give this bitch-ass dude what he deserves." Maurice looked at both his of friends. "I'm not going out like a sucka. I'm going at dude hard."

"I've never seen you this mad before. Be careful," J.B. ended.

❋　❋　❋

Maurice stood on the corner of his block right outside the twenty-four hour market, waiting for Brian to come pick him up. In his mind, he thought about the gruesome crime he was about to commit. He was a little nervous, but he knew that when it was over, he'd be respected by Tia and his crew.

Maurice anticipated the feel of the gun and how loud the gun-shots would be. He even questioned himself about really being able to go through with it, but him wanting to, outweighed him not wanting to just slightly. He knew this very act could lead to more and more crimes, and ultimately, his downfall.

All of his buddies had killed somebody, with the exception of J.B. Troy had killed Doug, a little over two years ago with Bandit, whom Maurice had always been skeptical about having for a friend. For some reason, he just didn't trust him. Even Brian, who wasn't a part of Maurice's crew, but a good friend nonetheless, had been convicted of first-degree murder as a juvenile.

Maurice looked down Sixth Street, and saw a white Saab 900, with a convertible top down, coming down the street. The car turned onto the Avenue, and Maurice walked across the street and got in.

Brian sat behind the wheel, with an angry expression on his face. "You ready?"

"Yeah," Maurice said. "You got a piece for me?"

Brian nodded. "I got a .357 for you, and a .38 for me."

"Let me hold it, so I can get the feel of it."

"Not yet," Brian told him. "Wait until we get a little closer to where we're goin'."

He drove slowly, as Maurice meditated on murder as they cruised downtown. There was a disturbing silence as they rode in the late hours of the night. The more Maurice thought about some guy pounding on his girl, the angrier he got.

Brian pushed a tiny button by the gearshift, and the black convertible top went up. He reached in the brown paper bag and pulled out a nickel-plated .357 Magnum revolver, and handed it to Maurice. Maurice took it, and looked at it as if it were a thing of beauty. A smile danced around his lips.

"It's loaded," Brian said.

Maurice was speechless as he examined the weapon. This was only the second gun he'd ever touched. Shortly after his ordeal of being kidnapped, he, Troy and J.B. had gone into a gun store out in Maryland, where they had the privilege of holding a 9mm. But the .357 in his hand now gave him mental joy, and a very secure feeling of invincibility.

Brian turned into the downtown neighborhood and stopped at a traffic light. "We're almost there," he said.

He reached into the bag to grab the snub-nosed black .38 caliber revolver. Gently, he placed the gun in his lap, holding on for dear life. It too was fully loaded.

He finally reached the efficiency apartments located on Ninth Street, and parked the car behind an old van.

"That niggah's car is right there," Brian said, pointing toward a red Mazda 929 that was parked across the street. "It's late.

Craig's probably not going out tonight, so we have to run up in his joint, so don't think about backing out."

Maurice looked at Brian. "How long should we wait before going up?"

"You wanna do it now?"

"Might as well," Maurice said, holding the handle of the gun tightly. He reached for the door handle.

"Wait," Brian said, grabbing Maurice by his shirt. "Look." He pointed toward the entrance of the apartment, as he saw a tall guy exiting. "Well, I'll be damned. There he is right there. Let's move."

Craig approached his automobile, dressed in a blue silk shirt and blue jeans. As he whistled, his left hand reached for his keys in his pocket. He thought he heard two car doors slam quickly, but he didn't pay it any mind.

Suddenly there was a loud boom. Craig fell to the ground, grabbing his arm. He looked around and spotted two men, as they fired several more times.

A bullet caught Craig dead on the bridge of the nose, as he tried to block the bullet with his forearm. Maurice and Brian ran up to him to make sure he was dead. As Brian quickly hurried back to his car, Maurice stood there looking at the fallen basketball star with a look of evil on his face.

❈ ❈ ❈

J.B. woke up bright and early the next morning. He slowly got out of bed and went into the bathroom to throw some water on his face. He was still high from the night before, but couldn't help thinking about when he'd be able to get his hands on some more weed. He went into the living room, grabbed the remote control, and turned on the television. He flipped through the channels, trying to find something to look at. Just then he looked at the television, and saw yellow tape that sealed off a D.C. street. He turned up the volume to listen.

"...Once again, this was the scene just six hours ago in downtown Washington," an anchorwoman for the morning news explained. "In case you're just now joining us, Georgetown basketball star, Craig Kenny, was gunned down outside his apartment building. This is a terrible tragedy. Police have no motive or suspects in the homicide..."

J.B. swallowed and shook his head. "No," he said quietly to himself. "Maurice didn't..."

He couldn't believe it. He half smiled as he shook his head, because the unlikeliest member in his crew had finally made the news.

Chapter Six

Maurice stepped into the sunlight wearing long, black shorts and a white tee. He walked to the edge of the patio and looked down at his mother who was in the backyard.

"Hey, Ma," he said.

Loretta looked up from watering her flower garden. "Good morning, baby."

Maurice seemed depressed, as he glared out at the sky with his hands behind his back. He tried not to think about what he'd done the previous night, but it was something he felt he had to do. He'd already read about the homicide in the paper, and it was the highlight of every news channel.

He turned and slid the patio door shut, as he stepped back into the house. He made it to the living room just as the doorbell rung. As Maurice opened the door, Troy and J.B. smiled like two proud parents. When Maurice looked at them, he could tell by the smiles on their faces they were aware of what he and Brian had done.

"What's up?" he said, greeting them.

"I didn't think you'd really do it," Troy told him. "I guess you proved us wrong."

Maurice smiled. "I told you."

"Well, since you're trigger happy now, come and do this robbery with us later on," Troy asked. "Those dudes on McDuffie Street are making loot, so we need to blitz those fools."

Maurice shook his head. "I'm not with all that robbing."

"Why, you scared?" Troy asked.

J.B. pulled out the article and handed it to Maurice. "From the looks of this, niggah, you ain't scared of nothing."

Maurice knew his friends were trying to pump him up, and force him to rob some guys who hadn't done anything to him. What they didn't understand was that he had a valid reason for killing Craig. He vowed to never rob a hustler because it reminded him of Lemar's situation a few years back.

"So, you gonna come with us or what?" Troy asked again.

Maurice shook his head. "I'm not robbing nobody," he responded.

"Boy, come take this trash out," they heard Loretta yell from inside the house.

"Look, I gotta go take care of that. I'll catch ya'll on the rebound." Maurice responded.

Troy looked at him with disappointment. "Yeah, we'll catch you later."

At that moment, J.B. stopped Troy as he turned around. "I'm gonna chill wit' Maurice for a minute."

"Whatever!" Troy responded, walking away with a slight attitude.

"Hi, J.B.," Loretta said, as they entered the house. "You look like you've lost a little weight," she lied, trying to make J.B. feel good about himself. People had always teased him about being an extra chubby teenager.

"Hi, Ms. Patterson," J.B. said, smiling at her. He always felt welcomed whenever he came over, because Loretta had taken a strong liking to him after he had informed the police a few years ago about the break-in at her house.

The two young men went into the kitchen and grabbed two bags of trash. Maurice knew J.B. wanted to know every detail about the murder. They walked outside to the patio, and down a flight of steps to the trash can.

J.B. looked at Maurice and smiled. "How did you kill him? What did you shoot him wit'? How did it feel to kill?"

by Mike C

"I'd rather not talk about it," Maurice retorted.

Shit, that means I took this trash out for nothing? J.B. thought.

※　※　※

J.B. stood on the corner with Troy, outside the twenty-four hour market, listening to his friend reminiscence, as daylight slowly vanished. Troy had been bragging nonstop about them successfully robbing Fat Ronald from McDuffie Street, for the second time. "Who says crime doesn't pay?" Troy joked. "That fat motherfucka had loads of money this time."

Troy reached in his back pocket and pulled out a dime bag of weed and a blunt. He removed the dried leaves from the blunt, and poured the weed inside. As he went to light it, he spotted a BMW coming slowly down the Avenue.

"Look J.B," Troy said.

J.B. looked up and immediately reached for his gun as he spotted the familiar car.

Troy also reached for his revolver. "I say we pop off right now!"

The car slowed down as J.B. pointed his weapon at the BMW. Carefully, he stared with a ruthless grimace, as his hand gripped the gun tightly. Suddenly, the car burned rubber, leaving marks in the street, as it swerved in the direction where J.B. and Troy stood. Shots rang out! Instantly, they both reacted by shooting wildly at the car, and running in a zig zag motion as the people in the car fired back. Troy's goal was to air the block out, but just as he realized he had no more rounds, the car raced down Seventh Street.

J.B. frowned. He looked back at Troy, who was checking the

empty chamber of his revolver.

"I see Fat Ronald wants revenge," Troy said, putting his gun away. He looked behind him and noticed the window of the store had been shattered with bullets. "Let's roll out before someone calls the police."

They both were silent as they walked down a dirty alley.

"Man, I say we go kill that niggah," Troy said.

J.B. looked at him for a second. "Well, we would have to kill his whole crew. Did you see how many of them were trying to get at us?" he responded.

"Then fuck it, let's get all of 'em."

J.B. nodded. "If we do that, I think we need another man. Let's ask Maurice to get involved."

Troy smirked. "Maurice ain't gonna do nothin'. What he did last night was a one-time thing."

"Nah, I don't think so. Something tells me it's in him now," J.B. replied. "Let's go to his house and see if he's home."

❈   ❈   ❈

Maurice sat on his porch, looking up and down his block. He wondered who'd gotten shot or killed on the Avenue, because moments ago, he'd heard a flurry of gunshots. This was normal in his hood.

His gaze moved to a small grassy area across the street where he saw Troy and J.B. walking in his direction.

Maurice stood and walked toward the steps, as J.B. and Troy crossed the street.

"What's up fellas?" Maurice asked.

"Everything," Troy responded. "We gotta go get those McDuffie Street dudes."

"For what?" Maurice asked, appearing to be irritated.

"They just shot at us," Troy said.

Maurice looked puzzled. "Why would they shoot at you?"

"Because we robbed Fat Ronald earlier today," Troy answered. "We took about thirteen thousand dollars from him, man."

"Are you serious? Man, you know those McDuffie Street dudes are gonna come after y'all," Maurice said.

"Which is why we gotta wipe them out," J.B. replied. He pulled his 9mm from under his shirt. He looked at Troy, then at Maurice. "You gotta help us get those fools."

Maurice smiled then shook his head. "Sorry, I can't. Ask Bandit to go with y'all."

"Bandit went to New York again. He'll be back tomorrow," J.B. responded.

"Come on, Maurice," Troy said. "Help us out on this one."

Maurice thought about things for a minute. He knew what his friends were asking him to do was wrong, but a part of him actually wanted to do it. For some reason, he'd gotten a slight high when he saw Craig's body drop. He wanted to experience that feeling again.

"So, what's up?" Troy asked again. "You gonna help us lay these fools down or what?"

Maurice looked at him. "I tell you what. Let's just shoot at them to let them know we can throw back."

"Fuck that, we gotta take them out before they take us out!" Troy shouted.

Maurice looked away, then back at Troy. "I'm down."

The moment he said that, his heart felt empty. It was if he was turning into someone else.

Troy smiled and slapped Maurice on the back. "Good lookin'

out, man. We'll ride up on McDuffie Street right now, that way they won't get a chance to get us back."

Maurice smiled. "Let's roll."

The three friends drove across town in a gray Volkswagon Jetta that Troy had stolen earlier. Maurice sat next to Troy, holding a black 9mm he'd gotten from one of J.B. associates. The gun felt much lighter than the .357 he carried the night before when he killed Craig. J.B. sat in the back, reloading a .45 caliber revolver. He reached in his pocket and placed the extra clip in his lap. He looked over at Maurice, who, like Troy, was quiet.

Soon they reached McDuffie Street. They drove suspiciously past Fat Ronald's house, and saw that his car was filled with bullet holes and a flat tire. *We fucked his car up earlier*, Troy thought. He circled the block a few times, as Maurice slapped the clip inside the 9mm.

"Maybe he ain't home," J.B. said.

"Well, we'll just have to wait and ambush 'em then," Troy said. He parked the car not too far from Fat Ronald's house, and slumped low into the seat. They all took turns keeping a close eye on the house. Three and a half hours later, there was still no sign of Fat Ronald or his crew.

Troy sat in the driver's seat with his eyes closed, while J.B. looked out the windshield at the target trying not to blink. Maurice became more impatient the longer they waited.

"I say we go get some weed, and come back," Troy suggested.

"Yeah, I'm wit' that," J.B. said, looking at Maurice. He knew his friend was going to disagree.

Just then a white Mercedes pulled up in front of Fat Ronald's house, and three guys got out. One of them appeared to be limping.

"Maybe the niggah limping got hit from one of our bullets earlier," J.B. said.

"It don't matter. Let's go," Troy replied, cocking his gun.

He opened the door, as J.B. jumped out the back. Maurice sat in the car, contemplating for few seconds before getting out. He then quietly opened the door, walked into the street nonchalantly, and took the lead in front of his buddies. They pulled their guns out, and tiptoed quickly to the sidewalk in front of the house where the three people stood. Troy recognized Fat Ronald as he reached for his house key to open the front door.

"What's up now, you fat motherfucka!" Troy shouted. Fat Ronald turned around in response to the voice.

Maurice raised a brow and shot at Fat Ronald, just as he was pissing in his pants from fear. *Look at his bitch ass*, Maurice thought, as Fat Ronald dropped to his knees, and was hit with an onslaught of bullets in his face.

Instantly, one of Fat Ronald's men charged at Maurice, but didn't get far, as three bullets from Troy's .45 took their toll. Troy walked over to him and knelt by his side. He grabbed the back of his head, placed the weapon in the man's mouth, and busted a single shot. "K-A-M, niggah, behind the trigger!" he yelled.

Maurice ran down the street behind J.B., who'd shot the other guy in the hamstring to slow him down. He fired another shot, which hit the guy in the back of the neck. The guy tripped over his feet and fell face first on the sidewalk. J.B. breathed heavily, as he fired two more times. He then pulled the trigger a final time, hitting the guy in the temple. Blood and brain tissue scattered everywhere. J.B. turned and saw Maurice running toward him. "Did Fat Ronald get dealt wit?" he asked.

"Yeah," Maurice said. "I...I got 'em," he huffed. "There's Troy, let's go!"

Young Assassin

Chapter Seven

Maurice had attended all his Friday morning classes, and was definitely ready for lunch when the bell rung. Although months had passed since Troy and J.B.'s beef with Fat Ronald, Maurice continued to think about the murders that came with it. He exited Coolidge High School through the rear, and walked through a large parking area to the sidewalk. He crossed the street, and walked toward a black-owned deli that served a variety of sandwiches.

As he got in line, he saw several people from school that he knew, but decided to give them all a nod. To Maurice, everyone at school was a loser, and conversation wasn't needed. He decided to wait outside until his order was ready.

As he looked around, he saw five guys and two girls walking toward the deli. He stepped out of their way to let them by, when one of the guys brushed up against his shoulder harshly. Maurice looked back for a moment, and saw the guy looking him up and down.

Maurice smiled, as he shook his head. *This fool must not know who he's dealing with,* he thought.

"You got a problem?" the guy asked.

Maurice looked at him, who he'd seen before. He figured he was a hustler, and from the looks of it, a troublemaker. Maurice eyed the gold chain with the diamond encrusted pistol charm around his neck.

"Come on man, leave that dude alone," another guy said.

"Good advice," Maurice responded. "You might want to listen to your friend."

"Fuck you!" the guy shouted, pushing him to the pavement.

Young Assassin

Maurice rolled over and sat up, after scrapping his left elbow. He stared at the guy and jumped to his feet, as rage ran through his body.

"What's up?" the guy asked, spreading his arms.

The four other guys tried to grab Maurice, but quickly stopped, as he pulled out a small Accu-Tek .25-caliber handgun from his pocket. He took the safety catch off and pointed the weapon directly toward his attacker. There was no need for senseless violence, but Maurice's anger wouldn't allow him to resist.

Suddenly, the handgun went off, and everyone scattered.

The guy fell to his knees, holding his chest. Anyone around stepped back. The guy tried to breathe carefully, as he lay on his side. Just as Maurice walked over, and put the gun to his head, he noticed a young girl looking him dead in his face. He didn't care.

Without hesitation, he fired again. "That's what's up, niggah!" he shouted.

"You didn't have to kill him!" one female bystander yelled to Maurice.

Maurice placed the gun in his pocket and walked away, without ever looking back. He strutted back to school with a slight grin, shocked at what he'd just done. *Shit, I didn't even get my sandwich,* he thought. The tiny bit of remorse he felt for what he'd just done, clearly didn't mess with his appetite. It was only his third time shooting someone, but it was starting to feel natural. Maurice didn't know what possessed him to shoot the guy in broad daylight, and in front of those people. He knew he was now in a world of trouble.

As he walked back to school, Maurice didn't know whether to leave or stay. If he stayed, he felt that would've been stupid. If he left, it would appear as if he was running, and that would seem suspicious. *Either way I'm screwed*, he thought. The people who saw him shoot that guy knew he went to Coolidge, since he'd seen some of them in the hallways countless times, and took classes with a few of them.

He slowly walked toward his fifth-period class. When he got to the end of the hallway, he turned the corner and spotted three D.C. policemen walking with two of the school security guards and the girl he'd seen earlier. Luckily, they didn't see him.

A shiver ran through him as he turned around and walked in the opposite direction. He spotted a girl's restroom and entered. After checking to make sure it was empty, he reached in his pocket and grabbed the small murder weapon. He removed the clip and placed it in a trashcan, before grabbing a roll of toilet paper to wipe his fingerprints off the gun, and wrap it in several layers.

Maurice walked over to the opened window, and threw the gun behind a group of bushes. "I'll come back and get it later," he said to himself, as headed out the bathroom with caution.

When Maurice walked into the classroom, he looked at the clock, and saw that he'd made it on time. He sighed, as he took his seat in the back of the room. The last thing he needed was to be sent to the office for tardiness, and risk running into the cops. Maurice's mind was clouded with thoughts of being locked up for a very long time, as one of his classmates read a section from their textbook.

He'd only been in class for ten minutes, when two security guards and the girl entered, followed by three D.C. police officers. Maurice looked up and stared at the six people, not knowing what was about to go down. He closed his eyes, took a deep breath, and looked toward the window.

"May I help you, officers?" the teacher asked.

One of the policemen stepped toward her, as Maurice turned his gaze from the window back to their direction. The officer looked very familiar. Maurice immediately recognized the mole on the side of his face. He'd seen him at the playground, along with Officer Bailey.

Young Assassin

"We're looking for an assailant, who's suspected of voluntary manslaughter," Officer Reynolds said to the teacher. He turned and gestured to the girl behind him. "This young woman witnessed the killing. We believe it was a student who attends this school. We've been searching each classroom, and…"

"There he is!" the girl shouted, cutting Reynolds off, as she pointed at Maurice.

Maurice remained calm, as fear flowed through his body. Both of the security guards and policemen looked in his direction.

"Are you sure?" one of the security guards asked.

The security guard was in doubt. *Maurice Patterson, the scholastic achiever, wanted for murder? I don't think so,* he thought.

"I'm positive," she answered. "He killed my friend."

"Are you're absolutely sure?" Officer Reynolds asked.

"I'm sure of it."

"Cuff him," Officer Reynolds ordered.

The students looked on in astonishment as two officers approached their classmate.

"I didn't kill anybody!" Maurice yelled.

One of the policemen grabbed him by the arm, as Maurice was pulled from his seat, while the other officer read him his rights.

As Tia walked down the hallway, toward the main office, thoughts of her precious little Donovan filled her head. She couldn't wait to return home to her son. The birth of one month old Donovan had filled her heart with so much joy, and she loved Maurice for being there with her the entire time she was pregnant. Not many guys would've stuck by her, especially with someone else's kid, but Maurice did. She knew he loved her, because he wouldn't have stayed with her this long if he didn't.

As she continued to walk toward the office, she heard what

sounded like loud footsteps coming from behind her. She turned around and saw a girl walking in front of three policemen, who happened to be escorting a student from the building. It was Maurice. Her eyes widened as she found herself walking toward him. Her walk quickly turned into a run, as to rushed to catch up with everyone.

"What happened?" Tia looked into Maurice's face. She didn't want to address him by his name. Growing up in the hood had taught her better.

"Get in touch with Brian for me," Maurice replied.

"But..."

"Just do it!" he said, raising his voice.

"Get out of our way, Miss," a policeman ordered. "This is official police business."

"Tia, what are you waiting for? Go!" Maurice yelled.

Tia moved out the way as the cops forced Maurice forward. She followed them outside, to a white paddy wagon. As the back doors were opened, Maurice looked at Tia before stepping inside. Seconds later, the truck headed out the parking lot.

❋   ❋   ❋

Lemar and Alvina were sitting on the sofa, in their birthday suits, when the telephone rang. Alvina got up and walked into the kitchen where the phone was.

When she answered it, a voice said, "Collect call from Maurice Patterson. Will you accept?"

Alvina frowned. *A collect call from Maurice?* "Yes, I'll accept," she said.

"Alvina, where's my brother?" Maurice asked, as soon as the line cleared.

"Hold on," she said, wondering where he was, and why he was calling collect. She called Lemar to the phone.

"Hello?" Lemar said.

"Lemar, I need help!"

"Maurice, where you at?"

"I'm pretty jammed up," Maurice responded.

"Jammed up where?" Lemar asked.

"Central Cell."

"Central Cell?" He frowned. "What are you doing in Central Cell?"

Maurice paused. He didn't want to let his brother down. "I got into some trouble."

"What kind of trouble?" Lemar asked, with a concerned response.

Alvina bit her fingernails after she heard Lemar's question.

"I really don't want to tell you," Maurice said, in a low voice.

"What do you mean you don't want to tell me? What are you doing in Central Cell?" Lemar asked for the second time.

Maurice paused again. "On a murder charge."

Lemar dropped the receiver and looked at Alvina, his eyes widening.

Alvina picked up the receiver. "Maurice, what's going on?" She watched as Lemar walked back into the living room.

"I'm in some trouble. That's all I can tell you."

"Maurice, talk to me," she pleaded.

Lemar quickly came back into the kitchen and snatched the phone out of her hand. "What am I suppose to tell Ma?" he asked.

"Make something up," Maurice ordered. "Tell her I ran away."

The thought of Maurice being sexually abused by other men went through Lemar's mind. His brother was tough, but not buffed enough to pull his weight in jail. He had been locked up enough to know that young boys had to prove themselves. "What else do you need?" Lemar asked.

"Right now, I need for you to try and reach a bail bondsman, then get me a lawyer. I know I'm going to be in here all weekend, so meet me at the District Courthouse early Monday morning," Maurice said, before hanging up.

Damn, I hate lying to my mother, Lemar thought, as he cleared the line to dial Loretta's number.

Young Assassin

Chapter Eight

Lemar appeared downtown at the District Courthouse, an hour before Maurice was to be arraigned on murder charges, along with his lawyer, Ryan Dalby. He hoped the judge would grant his brother bail so he could come home. If not, Lemar would have to tell his mother the truth about Maurice's whereabouts. That would be a hard thing to do, especially since she felt that Maurice was so good and innocent.

Lemar walked into the courthouse and saw a police officer standing with a metal detector in his hand. He stepped toward the officer, and emptied his pockets before being patted down. The procedures instantly reminded him of the day he turned himself in on drug charges. He took an escalator up two flights and waited in a long hallway for his brother to arrive.

Thirty minutes later, Maurice was escorted by two police officers to a courtroom on Level A. From where Lemar stood, Maurice looked to be very tired. Lemar and Ryan followed the officers and Maurice inside the small courtroom.

Lemar felt bad for his brother, as he watched one of the officers unlocked the cuffs, and lead Maurice to one of the tables.

"Well, let me work my magic," Ryan said to Lemar.

Ryan walked to where Maurice sat, and tapped the young man lightly on the shoulder. Maurice looked at him and swallowed. His expression pleaded for Ryan to get him out. Maurice turned around and spotted Lemar standing by the door in the rear. He nodded his head, before turning back around.

"I'll try to get the judge to consider bail, to avoid you waiting behind bars for a trial date." Ryan stated.

Maurice looked at him with exhaustion. "How you gonna do that?"

Ryan looked at him and smiled. "You'll see."

Brian found his way to the courtroom and saw Lemar standing by the door. "What's up, Lemar?" Brian said, noticing the fear in Lemar's eyes.

"What's up, Brian? What are you doing here?"

"I came to bail Maurice out."

"Thanks, but I'll take care of it," Lemar replied. "That's if the judge considers bail."

At that moment, the judge approached the bench with a folder full of papers. She picked up the gavel and banged her desk three times.

Maurice smiled, as he looked at the black female judge. *Maybe she'll go light on me*, he thought.

"Maurice Patterson, you've been charged with voluntary manslaughter while armed. How do you plead?"

Maurice yawned, "Not guilty."

"Well, unfortunately, you'll be sent to the D.C. jail to await trial," the judge replied.

"Excuse me, Your Honor," Ryan interrupted. "I have my client's high school transcripts to present to the court. He's a brilliant honor roll student, at Calvin Coolidge High School. I ask that you do not deny his request for bail, for the sake of him working toward his high school diploma."

Maurice smiled. *So that's how Ryan is going to take care of the situation.*

"Let me see his transcript," she replied.

Ryan approached the bench, and handed Maurice's transcript to the judge. She took the paper and studied it carefully. She nodded, as if she was impressed by Maurice's academic history.

The judge gazed at Ryan before speaking. "Straight A's, huh?" She paused before continuing. "I'll consider bail at thirty thousand dollars. Maurice Patterson, you'll still be taken to the D.C. Jail until bail can be paid. I'll write a statement to take with you." She slammed the gavel twice and handed the transcript back to Ryan.

A police officer approached Maurice and cuffed him, as Ryan approached.

"Thanks, Ryan," Maurice said smiling.

Ryan returned the expression. "Don't mention it."

"Here's the statement to give to the bondsman," the judge stated. "You'll need that, along with the receipt, when you go get the defendant."

Ryan took the document, and walked toward the rear of the courtroom. Brian and Lemar looked on as two officers escorted Maurice out the courtroom.

"Well, I guess there's nothing to do now, but pay his bail," Brian said.

Lemar nodded. "I guess so."

"I have until April to get this together," Ryan said, joining them. "Here's the written statement from the judge to take to the jail when you go and get him." He handed the paper to Lemar.

"Thanks a lot, Ryan. I'll send you a check in the mail."

Ryan smiled. "Okay, I'll see you later," he responded, as he walked out the courtroom.

"You think there were any witnesses?" Brian asked.

"There had to be," Lemar responded. "The news said that Maurice was arrested inside the school. Someone had to snitch on him."

"But the question is, who?"

"I don't know," Lemar said. "But I wish I did."

Brian looked at him. "Would you have the person who snitched killed, if you ever found out?"

Lemar shook his head. "Nah, something more of a compromise is my style. Besides, I'd never tell anyone if I were going to commit murder."

"Compromise? What you gonna do, bribe witnesses?"

Lemar looked at Brian and smiled. "Exactly. It could save a lot of bloodshed."

Brian wanted to respond to that, but didn't. He remained quiet, as he and Lemar walked out of the courthouse.

After Lemar paid the bail, he went to the D.C. jail to get his brother. He parked his car in the parking lot and thought about Seth as he entered, wishing he could get him out of jail too. Lemar grinned when he saw a fat woman with a tight guard uniform sitting in a glass booth. *She's two cupcakes away from a heart attack*, he thought. He walked over to her and slid the bail receipt and the written statement from the judge under the small opened space at the bottom.

"What's the prisoner's name?" she asked.

"Maurice Patterson," Lemar replied. "He was brought in here about an hour ago."

She picked up the phone and made a call. "He'll be exiting through the back gate. It'll take about ten minutes for him to be processed," she said, after hanging up.

Lemar smiled at the woman and walked back to his car. He drove around to where the back gate was located, and listened to the radio, as he waited for his little brother to come out.

"What's taking so long," he said, looking at his watch.

After waiting in his car for thirty minutes, he looked to his right and saw Maurice walking quickly toward him. He couldn't help, but notice his baby brother's swagger. A walk that indicated he was no longer a little kid. Lemar opened the door, and Maurice got in.

"What's up, bro?" Lemar said, in a disappointing tone.

Maurice looked at his older brother as they drove off. "What's up?"

"So, did you murder that dude?" Lemar asked immediately.

He wasn't interested in any small talk at the moment.

"Yeah, I killed him. He was trying to bully me, and I wasn't having it. He embarrassed me in front of a lot of people, so he had to get dealt with."

Lemar couldn't believe what he was hearing. *When did my little brother become such a gangsta,* he asked himself. "Where did you get a gun from?" Lemar asked. He pulled over to the side of the road to look at Maurice.

"Brian gave it to me," he answered sarcastically.

"What for?"

"Cause sometimes I need to have a gun on me," Maurice responded.

"Why?"

"For protection! Look at the shit that happened on Friday. If that dude had forced me to fight him, then his boys would've jumped in, and I would've gotten my ass kicked. I warned the dude to back up off me, but he took me for a sucker, so I had to lay his ass down. He pushed me into killing him."

Lemar remained silent for a moment. "Have you killed anybody else?"

Maurice paused for a few seconds. He didn't want to answer that question.

"You've killed more people, haven't you?"

"Yeah," Maurice answered. He couldn't even look at Lemar.

"How many people, Maurice?"

He shrugged his shoulders. "Two," Maurice replied. "My first body was Craig Kenny."

"You killed Craig Kenny?" Lemar asked, as his eyes widened.

"Me and Brian did," Maurice replied. "He hit my girl, Tia when she went to confront him about child support."

"So the baby that Tia had was Craig Kenny's?"

Maurice nodded. "Yeah."

Lemar shook his head in disbelief.

"Thanks for coming to get me," Maurice said, trying to change the subject.

Lemar didn't respond, as he pulled back into traffic. "Do you know if somebody snitched on you?"

"Yeah, some girl that was with the dude," Maurice replied.

"You know if she testifies against you, you could get a lot of time."

Maurice looked out the side window. "Then something has to be done about her."

Again, Lemar was in shock. He had no idea where Maurice could have gotten his brutal mentality from. He drove slowly, as a hundred thoughts passed through his mind. *Maybe I should've been a better influence.* He knew he couldn't allow Maurice to go to prison. It would upset his mother too much, so he had to prevent that from happening.

He turned to look at Maurice, who was still looking out the window. He knew his innocent brother had been transformed into a wild juvenile. Maurice had reached that stage in his young life, when one becomes vulnerable to his environment. Lemar wanted to tell Maurice that killing people wasn't cool, but he couldn't tell him that, while he was still doing wrong himself. All he could do was hope that Maurice would be careful out there, and realize the consequences of his actions.

They remained silent for the rest of the ride home.

After making a cup of hot herbal tea, Loretta walked into the living room. She put the cup down on the cocktail table, opened the front door, and grabbed the Washington Tribune from off the front porch.

by Mike G

After shutting the door, Loretta walked over to the sofa and picked up her tea. She placed the newspaper down on the table, leaned forward, and looked down at the huge article on the front page entitled: SUSPECT MAKES BAIL AFTER HEARING.

Loretta took a sip of her tea, as she began to read the article. She quickly learned that it was about a young man who'd been gunned down a few blocks from Coolidge High School. By the time she reached the second paragraph, she frowned as she read the name of the prime suspect -- Maurice Patterson of Milburn Street, Northwest, D.C. She swallowed, as a shiver ran straight through her like a run away freight train.

Loretta continued to read the story, with her heart pounding like a drum inside her chest. After she finished, she stood up and hurried upstairs to Maurice's bedroom with the newspaper in hand. Loretta pushed the door open and turned on the light. Maurice was sleeping peacefully. She walked over to his bed and shook him forcefully.

"Maurice, get up! Get your ass up now!" She hit him on the arm with the newspaper.

Suddenly his eyes opened. He looked up and saw his mother glaring down at him. "What's the matter?" he asked.

"Tell me the truth about where you were last weekend," she demanded. "I want the truth. Don't lie to me, Maurice."

"I told you I went on a trip to New York with some of my classmates," he said, sitting up.

"That's a bunch of bullshit, Maurice! The real reason you weren't home is because you were locked up, isn't it?"

Maurice looked at Loretta with a sad stare. He couldn't lie to his mother anymore. "Yeah, I was taken into custody as a suspect for killing someone, but I didn't do it!"

"Well, if you didn't do it, then why would that girl tell the police that you did?"

There was a long pause. He was wondering where she had gotten this information. He knew Lemar or Alvina hadn't told her.

"Well?" Loretta asked.

"Well, what?"

"If you didn't do it, then why would that child lie on you?"

Maurice took a deep breath. "I didn't kill anybody Ma," he responded.

"Why am I having trouble believing you?" She put the newspaper in front of him. "If you didn't kill anybody, why would they put your name in the paper as the prime suspect?" she asked, pointing to the article.

Maurice grabbed the paper, while sneaking a look at her. As he read the article, he became even more concerned. *So, this is where she got her information,* he thought. *Why did they put this shit in the paper?* He stared at the drawings on his wall. "You have to believe me. I didn't kill anybody," he said again.

"If you can tell me the reason why someone would pick you out of everybody else at your school, then maybe I'll believe you. The article says that girl told police the boy was trying to start a fight with you, and then you shot and killed him."

"I was falsely implicated," he replied, with confidence.

She shook her head. "Did you kill that boy, Maurice?" Loretta asked, raising her voice.

Maurice swallowed and scratched the top of his head. He wondered if his telling her the truth would change their relationship, just like her relationship with Lemar had changed when she first found out he was a drug-dealer.

"Yeah, I killed him," he answered in a low tone.

Loretta turned her back to him, as tears rolled down her face. Maurice stared at his mother's back. He couldn't believe he'd broken his promise to never hurt her.

"Ma, I'm sorry."

"Save your apology," Loretta told him. "I'm just thinking about how that boy's mother must feel." She turned to look at him. "I knew there was something going on with you. I saw you changing right before my eyes." She looked down and shook her head, as tears fell on the floor. "I should've known you were falling by the wayside. You've done a despicable act."

"He was trying to fight me," Maurice said defensively. "I gave him a warning to leave me alone, and he refused, so I shot him."

"That's no excuse to kill a human being!" she shouted. "You're no longer welcome here. I want you to pack your belongings and get out."

"Ma, you sound like a radical," Maurice said.

Loretta looked at him with an evil expression. "What did you call me?" She walked over to him and slapped his face, as her tears continued to fall. "Now, get the hell out of here!"

Maurice got out of bed and looked at her, in disbelief. He went into his hamper and reached for a dirty pair of blue jeans. After putting them on, he went into his closet, grabbed a gray hooded vest, and a pair of white Nike tennis shoes.

Maurice looked at Loretta, who looked as if she wanted to strike him again.

"I'm gone," he told her. The sullen look on his face defining his disgust, as well as the hurt he felt.

"Then go!" she hollered.

Maurice ran down the stairs, and slammed the front door as hard as he could after stepping into the mean streets.

Young Assassin

Chapter Nine

The sirens screamed loudly from atop a D.C.P.D. squad car. Its driver was in hot pursuit of two black males, running relentlessly on foot down a residential sidewalk.

"This is Unit A-Fifty-Seven," Officer Bailey said into his radio. "We're pursuing two black males, who ran from us after we spotted them distributing crack cocaine. They just ran into an alley near the intersection of Eighth and Kalhoun Avenue on the Twenty-One-Hundred block."

Bailey turned into the alley, smashing his foot on the accelerator, as he clutched the black automatic handgun in his holster.

"One man is wearing an all-black sweatsuit with white sneakers, and the other is wearing black pants and a white football jersey."

"Ten-four, this is Unit A-Sixty-Six," the police response said. "We're not too far from where you are. We'll be there right away."

Officer Reynolds sat beside Officer Bailey, with his heart beating rapidly. "Don't let them get away, partner," he said.

Up ahead, one of the men hopped over a fence into someone's backyard and disappeared, while the other kept straight up the alley. "It looks like we've lost one," Reynolds said. "Make sure you don't lose the one in front of us."

He took the CB from out of Bailey's hand. "A-Sixty-Six, this is A-Fifty-Seven again. The suspect wearing an all black sweatsuit and white sneakers has fled over a fence and into a backyard. He's headed toward Van Buren Place."

"Ten-four, A-Fifty-Seven."

The man running in front of them seemed to be slowing down a bit. He came out the other end of the alley, ran across the street, and down another residential sidewalk.

Officer Bailey whipped the automobile out the alley, back onto the street, and headed down to the point where he would meet up with the young man. He grabbed the gun from his holster, and flicked on a switch that activated his loudspeaker.

"Stop, or I'll shoot!" he shouted.

"You don't really mean that, do you?" Reynolds asked.

Bailey switched off the loudspeaker. "Yes, I do." He switched it back on again. "This is my last warning! Surrender or be prepared to get shot!"

Despite Bailey's commands, the man kept running. As he came to the end of the sidewalk, he heard four shots fired, and then a squad car slamming on brakes. Trying to get away, the man attempted to run across the street, but ran right into the police car door, and fell to the ground. Officer Reynolds got out the car and went after the man, who tried to get up and run. But Reynolds was already on top of him, reaching for his cuffs.

Bailey walked to where his partner had the suspect on the ground, with a knee in his back. After Reynolds forced the man up off the ground, Bailey punched him in the stomach.

"I gave you a warning to halt. Not only am I charging you with distribution of crack cocaine, but I'm also nailing your ass for resisting arrest."

The man looked at Bailey, then peeked down at the black firearm he was holding by the barrel. Bailey lifted the gun up and struck the suspect across the face twice with the handle.

"Bailey, no!" Reynolds yelled. "We have him now. Cool down some." Reynolds was starting to get frustrated and was in need of his daily drink. Vodka and Tonic was his daily ritual, one glass before his shift stared, and one after it ended. Sometimes he even snuck one in while on duty.

"He shouldn't have run away from me when I ordered him to stop," Bailey said. "Put this lousy scum in the squad car."

The man's face was bruised from the blows Bailey had inflicted on him. He felt anger and regret for getting caught. He spit in Bailey's face and kicked him in the thigh, as Reynolds walked him to the squad car.

Bailey looked at the man angrily, and held his leg. He quickly limped back to the car, and opened the back door. Instantly, Bailey took his club, and swung it toward the suspect's head.

"Jesus, Bailey!" Reynolds shouted.

Bailey didn't pay any mind to what his partner had to say.

"Motherfucka, I'm going to kill you for spitting in my face!" he screamed at the man, as he raised the nightstick high above his head.

Maurice was on the move, with drugs and a firearm in his possession. He had climbed over a fence and into someone's backyard, after he and J.B. were spotted selling drugs on the Avenue. He moved through the yard with an athletic swiftness, and ran between two houses, to come out on the other side.

As he ran down Van Buren Place, he spotted a police car heading up the block the wrong way. The vehicle stopped, and an officer rolled his window down.

"Freeze right there!" he heard a voice say from a megaphone. "Cooperate, and we'll be your friend. Not complying will be your end."

"What is that, a fake ass rhyme?" Maurice said to himself. He continued to run as a policeman got out of the vehicle. He heard the officer's footsteps tapping against the concrete. Maurice looked behind him, determined to shoot the officer, if that's what it took to get away.

Maurice hoped that J.B. had gotten away from the other officers, or that he was fighting with every ounce of energy he had in order not to get caught. He also hoped his face hadn't been seen by the police.

Suddenly, he saw the squad car going down the street in

reverse, in a desperate attempt to capture him. Two shots were fired from the officer chasing him on foot. One barely missed Maurice, scraping past the sleeve of his jacket, and burning a slight hole in it. The other shot clearly missed.

Maurice removed the silver and black 10mm from his jacket, took the safety catch off, and fired a couple shots back, striking the officer in the chest and below the stomach. The officer fell to the pavement. Without remorse, Maurice continued to sprint as fast as he could, his strength failing, as he pushed himself to the very limit his body would allow.

He quickly ran through someone's front yard, exited through a gate that led to a backyard, and ended up in the alley. Maurice unzipped the black hoody he had on, and tossed it in a nearby garbage can. He knew the cop driving saw him enter the gate, and would be coming into the alley any second. On top of the jam he was in, he was also awaiting trial for manslaughter, a charge that could land him in jail for at least twenty years.

After being put out his mother's house six months ago, he hadn't returned, let alone called to see how she was doing. Maurice had turned to nickel and dime drug sales in order to support himself. He'd moved into Courtney's basement, a long time friend of the family, and paid her rent to stay there. Even she had begged him to go back home and talk things over with his mother, but Maurice didn't want to go back. He was satisfied where he was, and felt it would be best to leave Loretta alone.

Maurice sucked in air as he leaned up against a gate, thinking of the best plan. He looked at the gun in his hand, and wondered if he should dump it someplace. He heard the sound of sirens screaming in his ears, as if they were right next to him.

Suddenly, he ran down the alley in the opposite direction of the sirens. Maurice hopped over yet another fence and looked around the backyard where he landed, hoping to find a hiding spot. He spotted a light green shed and decided to hide there, as he sucked in the cool wind.

The squad car sped past the backyard, and Maurice instantly sighed.

Half of Unit A-Sixty-Six patrolled around for ten minutes, before driving back up to Van Buren Place. A short, hunched-back senior citizen, with white hair and thick glasses came over to one of the squad cars.

"Officer," he said, "a policeman over there is badly wounded. I've already called for an ambulance." He pointed to the side-walk, where people were crowded around.

The officer reached for his CB. "This is Officer Brown, Unit A-Sixty-Six to dispatch. Officer Nelson is down. I repeat...Officer Nelson is down! I need an ambulance. Please hurry!"

"Ten-four," the dispatch said. "Exact location, Officer Brown?"

"I'm on the 6200 block of Van Buren Place."

Officer Brown rushed through the crowd of people. "Excuse me, officer coming through."

As Brown approached, Nelson heard the familiar voice of his partner. "Brown, I'm hit," he moaned, gasping for air.

"You'll be okay," Brown said to him.

"A bullet hit the side of my throat," he said, with a squeal in his tone. "I can't breathe."

"Hang on, Nelson," he said. "Don't die on me, man." When his partner didn't respond, Brown feared the worst. "Nelson!" he yelled.

Nelson still didn't respond. Just then two ambulances showed up, one after another. Brown knew they were too late to save his partner's life.

❋   ❋   ❋

Young Assassin

J.B. sat in a small cell of the Fourth District Precinct, wondering if Maurice had gotten away from the police.

At that moment, a police officer appeared. He unlocked the cell and walked in, as another officer stood outside, with paper and clipboard.

"I'm Sergeant McLain. I'm going to ask you some simple questions, and I want simple answers. What's your name?"

"Jerome Barnes," J.B. answered.

"Social Security number?

"Umm...one-two-one-seven-nine-two-six." J.B. lied, and he knew it wasn't enough numbers. *They're probably too stupid to figure that out,* he thought.

The officer frowned. "Now, what's the other person's name who was selling drugs with you?"

J.B. would never betray any of his buddies -- especially to the police. "I don't know who he was." he said, hunching his shoulders.

McLain walked over to J.B, grabbed him by the collar of his football jersey, and slammed him into the wall. He spit in J.B.'s face.

"You listen to me, you punk! Whoever that person was shot and killed a very, very good cop from out of this district! I want his name!"

"I don't know his name," J.B. answered.

"Tell me his name!" the sergeant demanded. He slammed J.B. up against the steel bars.

"I told you, I don't know his name!" J.B. screamed.

"You know what?" McLain said to him. "I'm going to see to it that the judge hits you with hard time. You wanna be charged with murder? I'll see to that!"

"You can't charge me with murder because I didn't kill nobody," J.B. said, being sarcastic.

McLain unloosened his grip on J.B.'s collar, and punched him

84

in the stomach. The youngster fell to his knees and clutched his body.

"But you know who did, punk! I want his name!"

"For the last time, I don't know his name!" J.B. said, as he looked up at the officer.

The sergeant slapped J.B.'s face, then turned around and faced the officer standing in front of the cell. "Did you get his name and social security number?"

"Yes, sir."

The sergeant turned around and looked at J.B. before walking out. "You're really gonna pay for this."

They walked to the elevator at the end of the hallway.

J.B. took a deep breath. *Maurice killed a cop? Damn!*

❋ ❋ ❋

Tia looked at Bonita strangely. She could swear her mother had lost at least fifteen to twenty pounds since the beginning of the school year.

"Momma, I've noticed dat you're losing weight."

Bonita turned from the window to look at her. "I'm on a diet."

"And you hardly ever sleep," Tia added.

Bonita kept quiet, wondering where Tia was going with this. She turned back around to look out the window. "I needed to lose weight," she replied.

"For what? You looked fine the way you were."

Bonita walked away from the window and went into the kitchen, as Tia followed. Tia was fed up with her mother's lies.

"Momma, I know a crackhead when I see one," she said.

"So what are you insinuating?" Bonita asked.

Tia sighed. "Momma, I'm not stupid. You're on drugs, aren't you?"

"No I'm not, for your information."

"Look me in the eye and tell dat to me."

Bonita turned and walked up in her daughter's face. "I'm not on drugs, Tia."

Tia looked at her mother, as Bonita turned and took a few steps toward the sink. She ran the water and reached inside the cabinet for a glass.

Tia grabbed her hand and spun her mother around. "I hope not, but by the way you look, it seems doubtful." She let go, and returned to the living room to sit on the couch.

"Don't put your damn hands on me again, Tia. I'm not the child," Bonita said, as someone knocked. She turned around and walked to the door. "Hey Maurice. Come on in."

"Hi, Ms. Clark," he replied, as he stepped into the apartment.

Maurice had been watching his back for the last hour after eluding the police. For now, he felt safe, because they hadn't seen his face, and didn't know it was him who'd killed the cop.

He walked over to Tia, who was now standing with her arms spread wide. He kissed her cheek, just in case her mother was watching.

"Maurice, I have somethin' important to tell you," Tia said.

He grabbed her hand, as they sat down on the couch. "What's up?"

Tia looked for her mother, who'd gone back into the kitchen, before she continued. "I'm pregnant, Maurice."

Maurice looked at her, as a distracted expression spread across his face. He turned away, then smiled as he returned her gaze.

"That's the best news I've heard all day!" he shouted.

"What the hell did you just say, Tia?" Bonita asked, as she walked back into the living room. "You're pregnant?"

Tia looked at her and nodded. Then she looked at Maurice. She had to tell him something else, but it was hard to say.

"Tia, you just had a baby," Bonita said.

"Momma, can I please talk to Maurice alone?"

"Whatever," Bonita said. "I'm not watching a bunch of damn kids!" She went to her bedroom and slammed the door.

"You don't seem happy." Maurice said.

"I'm so sorry, Maurice, but I can't have this baby."

He frowned. "Why the fuck not?"

"I'm still young, and I can't endure being the mother of two kids right now. Besides, I don't think you're ready to be a father."

Maurice understood, but didn't agree. "So, what are you going to do, get an abortion?"

"Yes."

"It's wrong, Tia," he said. He shook his head, as he bit his bottom lip, and clinched his fists.

"I know it's wrong, but I'm not ready for any more kids right now."

"It's wrong," he said again.

"I know, and I'm sorry."

"I don't fucking believe you," Maurice said, raising his voice a little bit.

"Okay, go on and make it sound like I'm such a terrible person because I wanna get an abortion." Tia looked away from him, and combed her fingers through her hair.

"Look, if you abort my kid, it's over between us."

"Don't even go there!" she said. "So, you would leave me if I actually went through with this?"

"You damn right. You had that niggah, Craig's baby, why can't you have mine. "

"Maurice, we can have children when we get older, but just not right now. Besides, Donovan is not even one yet."

"I see what's going on. I was good enough to help your broke ass take care of a son that's not even mine, but I'm not good enough to take care of my own child. Tia, if you get rid of my baby, it's over," he repeated.

Just then Tia heard Donovan crying from the back room. She got up and faced Maurice. "I've already scheduled a seven o'clock appointment tomorrow."

Suddenly, Brian came through the door, wearing a grin and a blue cap turned backwards on his head. Tia left the room to go check on Donovan.

"What's up?" Brian said, when he closed the door and saw Maurice.

"What's up, Brian?" Maurice answered.

Brian studied him. "What's wrong, man?'

"Nothing at all."

Brian went into the dining room and sat at the table, as Maurice walked over to the door. "Where you goin'?" he asked.

"Home," Maurice replied.

Tia appeared with Donovan wrapped in her arms, as Maurice headed for the door.

"Hey, Brian," she said.

"What's up, sis?" he responded. "So, Maurice, you want me to take you home?"

Maurice stopped and turned around. "Yeah, take me home, man."

Tia walked over to Brian. "Can you hold up a minute? There's somethin' I need to bring to your attention."

Maurice interrupted. "Brian, I'll be waiting outside by your car." He opened the door and walked out, without saying anything else to Tia.

"What?" Brian asked, biting into an orange.

"It's about Ma'ma," she whispered. "I think she's on drugs."

"She is," Brian said bluntly.

"What? You know already?" Tia looked shocked.

"Yeah, she and Reverend Tate are having an affair," he replied. "Both of 'em be smoking rocks."

"You don't even seem to care," she said, in a vicious tone.
Brian looked up at her. "I don't!"

"Why? She's your mother!"

"Look, I ain't puttin' the pipe in her mouth," Brian responded.

"But you can try to turn her away from smoking dat shit! You don't even love her, do you?"

"Look, I don't have time to help somebody who don't wanna be helped, Tia. Crack is the devil's love potion. When it has you, you're had."

"Dat's such an insensitive thing to say, Brian."

"Look, Maurice is waitin' for me," he said. He ate the remainder of the orange in his hand, and stood up.

"I don't believe you. You don't care because you're a stone cold hustler. You're just in it for the money."

"Money is all dat's worth caring about," he replied.

Tia was tempted to slap his face from the nasty comment. Instead, she looked at him with malice and walked away. Brian got a paper towel from the kitchen, and hurried out the door to catch up with Maurice.

Young Assassin

Chapter Ten

As Maurice walked out of the corner store, he heard a voice call his name from behind. He turned and looked down the Avenue. He saw someone approaching, and wondered who it could be. Suddenly, he saw Bandit, who was dressed in a money-green Le Coq Sportif sweatsuit, with a wad of cash in his left hand.

Maurice nodded. "What's up?"

"Nothin' much," Bandit replied. "I need you to do a favor for me."

"What?"

"I need you to come with me over to Northeast and smoke this fool."

"Who, a hustler?" Maurice asked with concern.

Bandit shrugged. "Who else would it be?"

"I don't do that contract shit," Maurice said, looking away.

"Look, I was paid three Gs to smoke this niggah," Bandit responded. "If you do this with me, I'll give you a G."

"A thousand?" Maurice asked. *It sounds reasonable, plus it'll take care of my rent for the next couple of months at Courtney's crib,* he thought. "Okay, I'll go with you."

They started walking toward Bandit's maroon Cherokee.

"Who is he?" Maurice asked, approaching the passenger side.

"This dude named Todd."

Todd? He thought he'd heard Lemar mention that name before, but he wasn't really sure.

Maurice and Bandit cruised to the Northeast portion of the city, and waited outside a populated apartment complex. A dangerous spot known for drugs and violence.

"I robbed Todd once," Bandit admitted. "He's a big-time drug-dealer that nobody likes." He pointed. "There's his Mercedes right there." Maurice looked and saw the car with shiny rims, Bandit was referring to.

"You said you robbed him once?"

"Yeah, in a J.C. Penney's parking lot a few years ago. Shot him three times in the chest too."

Just then a man stepped out of the Mercedes, wearing a bright red jacket.

"Is that him?" Maurice asked.

"Yeah."

Maurice spun the chamber of his revolver, making sure he had a full load of rounds. As Bandit reached in the back and grabbed the shotgun, Maurice stepped out the truck boldly.

"Wait a minute," Bandit called out, but Maurice had closed the door, headed toward the target.

Bandit watched as Maurice ran up to the man without fear, and shot him twice in the chest. The man stumbled and dropped. Maurice stepped back, aimed at his head, and shot three bullets into his skull, then hurried back to the truck and hopped in.

"I told your ass to wait a minute!" Bandit shouted, pulling off.

"The hell with that! What the fuck were we waiting for, Christmas?" Maurice asked. "He's dead. Now, gimme my money."

Bandit shot Maurice a strange look. *I had no idea Maurice was laying people down like that. I might need to keep an eye on that niggah*, he thought.

❉   ❉   ❉

Troy walked up and down the Avenue. There was no sign of

Maurice. He reached into the pocket of his blue hoody and got the fat blunt he'd rolled before he came out the house. He reached in his pants pocket, pulled out a book of matches, and lit the blunt. He took several puffs, then swallowed the smoke and coughed uncontrollably. Smoking weed had always been his favorite pastime, but his lungs were surely suffering by now.

As the cold wind shoved him back a little, Troy realized he was ready to go back inside. With J.B. locked up, and Maurice awaiting a murder trial, Troy knew there was a chance the Kalhoun Avenue Mob was in jeopardy; even if it was only for a hot second. He knew that J.B. would be getting out one day, but if Maurice was thrown in jail, that was it for him. Although Bandit was their leader, Maurice was more respected, he never boasted about how ruthless he was.

Just then, Troy saw a truck park across the street. He watched as Maurice and Bandit stepped out and walked over to where he was.

"Where did you go?" he asked Maurice. "What's up, Bandit?"

"Nothin' much," Bandit said, as he reached in his pocket. He counted out a thousand dollars and handed it to Maurice.

Maurice grabbed the money, put it in his jacket pocket, and looked at Troy. "Did you talk to J.B.?"

"Yeah, right before I called you," Troy replied. "What happened anyway?"

Maurice informed Troy and Bandit about the details of what happened earlier that day, and how he'd killed the cop.

"You're becoming a real thorough dude, Maurice," Bandit said. "You did something I've never done. You actually killed a police officer."

"I did what I had to do," Maurice responded nonchalantly. "Plus the cop shot at me first. I wasn't trying to kill him."

By now Troy had finished the remainder of the blunt, and threw the roach into the grass.

"I'm out," Bandit announced, as he walked toward the truck.

"I was thinking," Troy said to Maurice, "what do you plan to do about that girl who's suppose to testify against you next month?"

"Lemar's gonna bribe her as soon as I find out where she lives," Maurice said. "If she doesn't take the money, then I'll just have to put my murder game down."

❋   ❋   ❋

Lemar had just arrived at his apartment after wheeling and dealing. He always spent a great amount of time on his cell phone, making deals with other hustlers, so he could make plenty of loot. It was always about serving kilos, and receiving thousands and thousands of dollars. It was a routine thing for him day in and day out.

Just as he was about to walk into the bedroom to check on Alvina, the phone rang. He hurried into the kitchen to answer it, just in case she was asleep. "Hello?"

"Lemar, what's up? Long time, no hear from, bro."

"What's up, Maurice? It's about time you called. How have you been? Ma is worried about you. She wants you to come back home. Where are you?"

"Chillin' on Kalhoun Avenue," Maurice told him.

"What you doing on Kalhoun?"

There was a short pause. "Just hanging out."

"Where you staying now?"

"Can't tell you that, Lemar," Maurice answered.

"Why? I'm not gonna tell Ma."

After contemplating for a few seconds, Maurice decided to give in. "I live with Courtney."

"I guess that's cool. Courtney is good people. Why you hanging out on Kalhoun Avenue?" Lemar asked again.

There was another short pause. "Hustling," Maurice responded reluctantly.

"I see. Just watch yourself out there in the street, boy," Lemar warned him. "Hustlers die every day."

"I'm not afraid to die," Maurice told him boldly.

Lemar smiled at the remark, then a frown appeared on his face. "Any word about that girl?" he asked.

Maurice was hoping that Lemar would get around to that.

"Not yet. I gotta find out her address and telephone number."

"Get someone to do it for you," Lemar suggested. "It wouldn't look too good if you got caught. You see what I'm saying?"

"Yeah, I understand."

"Look, I gotta go. Be careful out there, bro. Page me tomorrow."

"I will."

Lemar hung the phone up and sighed. He walked out the kitchen, went into the bedroom, and turned on the light. He smiled, as he saw Alvina lying under the royal purple silk sheets on their queen-sized bed. She opened her eyes and looked up at him seductively.

"Hey," he said, as he watched her remove the sheets.

"Hi," she replied. "Lemar, I have something to ask you."

"I have something I wanna ask you too."

He sat down on the bed, and he looked into her sleepy eyes.

"You first," Alvina said.

"No, you first."

"Lemar, I...." Alvina yawned and fell back onto the pillows. She closed her eyes. "I'll ask you tomorrow," she said. A few seconds later, she was snoozing silently.

Lemar removed his gaze from her and snapped his fingers.

"Damn," he whispered to himself. "Of all nights, she had to fall asleep."

Young Assassin

He removed his clothes and threw them on the floor before climbing into bed.

❋   ❋   ❋

When Lemar woke up the next morning, he saw that Alvina had already left the house. He got up out of bed, went into the bathroom and looked into the mirror, noticing that he needed a haircut. He smiled, as he thought, *here I am, twenty-three years old, in love, and ready to ask the love of my life to marry me. Life is good.*

He went to the front door and grabbed the latest edition of the Washington Tribune. After closing the door behind him, Lemar turned on the television, sat on the floor, and opened the paper.

As he reached the Metro section, he came across an article entitled, MAN IS GUNNED DOWN ON NORTHEAST SIDE-WALK.

Lemar read the article, and to his surprise, the victim was someone he not only knew, but had done business with a few times. He shook his head, *another damn funeral I gotta go to.*

He sighed and flipped to the sports section. Just before he could read about the NCAA basketball tournament, someone knocked on the door. Lemar got up, wondering who it could be.

When he opened the door, he saw the gloomy face of his brother. "Maurice, what are you doing here," Lemar asked.

Maurice looked into his brother's cool stare. At that moment, he realized how much he idolized his big brother. "I need to talk to you." He forced a smile as he stepped in.

Lemar closed the door behind him. "What's going on?" He knew something had to be wrong.

"Tia told me she's pregnant, but isn't gonna have the baby.

That pissed me off so bad, I told her if she goes through with an abortion, I'm leaving her ass." Maurice said, sitting on the sofa.

"Damn, when is she supposed to do that?"

"At seven."

"That was a few hours ago," Lemar responded, also realizing that Maurice should have been in school. "You think she got it done?"

"I don't know. I hope not. I know if I see her, I might go off."

Lemar laughed, but knew it wasn't funny. "If I were you, I'd just find someone else. You're young. You have plenty of time to have a family."

Maurice shook his head. He wanted to hurt Tia for making the decision to kill his baby. "So, what's been up with you?" he asked, changing the subject.

"I'm gonna ask Alvina to marry me," Lemar said, as a joyous expression appeared on his face. "I wanted to ask her last night, but she fell asleep."

"I hope things work out for you," Maurice replied. "Alvina is like a sister to me."

"Thanks, bro," Lemar said, sitting next to Maurice. He contemplated about changing the subject, but he knew it had to be done. "Listen, I don't want you selling drugs, man. And why aren't you in school?"

Maurice knew this conversation would come up sooner or later. "I don't have to be at school until third period. You know I'm a senior now, so I don't have many classes." He faced Lemar man to man. "Look, I hate to disappoint you about selling drugs and all, but I gotta do what I gotta do. I'm not a little kid anymore. I'll always be your little brother, but I'm my own man now. I gotta develop my own identity."

"What you trying to say, Maurice?" Lemar asked.

"Respect the decisions I make."

"Oh, so should I respect the fact that you're out here killing people?"

"Yeah, you should," Maurice replied sarcastically. "As a matter of fact, I just killed some dude last night."

Lemar couldn't believe what was going on. "Who? Where?" he asked in shock.

"Over in Northeast," Maurice responded. "It was some dude named Todd."

Lemar thought back to the article he'd just read. He placed the paper on Maurice's lap. "What in the hell is wrong with you? Are you killing niggahs for money now?"

"I let Bandit talk me into it." Maurice lowered his head, as Lemar looked at him with harsh disapproval.

"I knew that dude!" Lemar shouted. "We used to roll together back in the day. Who wanted Todd dead?"

"I think some kingpin type dude. Bandit said he robbed and shot Todd a few years ago outside a J.C. Penny's parking lot."

Lemar's eyes widened. "He did what?"

Damn, didn't he just hear what I said? Maurice thought. "He told me that he robbed the dude, Todd, a while back. What's the big deal?"

Lemar turned around, and then faced his brother. "The big deal is I was with Todd the day he was robbed and shot in the parking lot. I was robbed too! And you know what else?"

Maurice studied him, frowning. "What?"

"I was forced to kill Doug because of that incident. It was Doug's drugs and money that Bandit and two other dudes took from me."

"Who's Doug?" Maurice asked.

"The fool who had you kidnapped. He was my supplier."

Maurice stood and walked over to the window, with the newspaper in his hand.

"You mean to tell me that I was kidnapped because of Bandit?"

"It looks that way," Lemar replied. "And to top it off, I paid Bandit to kill Doug."

"Bandit's mother might as well pick out his fucking casket because he's a dead man," Maurice said, as he anger grew. He stood up and paced back and forth. Suddenly, he stopped and looked at Lemar. "Oh, and I found out the girl, who's going to testify against me is named, Veronica Russell. So, that's two people who need to go."

Young Assassin

Chapter Eleven

Lemar looked out across the Avenue as he drove to his mother's house. On his way, he saw people pulling their cars over to buy drugs, and crackheads were everywhere. His old neighborhood had become so infested with drugs it made Lemar ashamed, and he knew that he was part of the problem.

As he turned off the Avenue, he noticed a squad car behind him. Lemar looked into his rearview mirror, trying to make out the face of the officer driving, but it was too far for him to see. Lemar smiled, wondering if he should drive a few more blocks, just to see if the nuisance would continue to trail him. Instead, he parked his car in a space right in front of his mother's house. He shook his head as the squad car drove past.

Police never have anything else to do, Lemar thought.

As he walked toward his mother's house, the door opened, and he saw Loretta smiling.

"Hey, sweetie. Come in." As Lemar bent over to hug her, she frowned. "I see you got another car. How much did that cost?" she asked, with her hands on her hips. "Should I be skeptical about letting your butt in here?"

"Cut it out, Ma," Lemar said, stepping inside. He decided to ignore her question about the car. "You should always let your son inside to come visit you." He kissed her on her cheek. "How are you?"

Loretta closed the door. "I'm doing okay. Still no word from your brother?"

Lemar walked in the kitchen, and looked in the refrigerator. He missed his mother's good cooking. "As a matter of fact, he stopped by my house this morning. He's doing just fine, Ma.

Don't worry about him," he said, putting a piece of turkey in his mouth.

"Where's he staying? Who is he staying with?"

"He doesn't want you to know, Ma. I'm sure he'll come back when he's ready. I know he still loves you."

Loretta smirked, as sorrow filled her heart. "Please, Lemar, tell me where he is."

"Ma, I told Maurice that I wouldn't tell you."

"Is he still in school?" Loretta asked.

"Yes." He looked away from her for a moment. "Ma, there are a few things about Maurice you should know."

"What?" Loretta asked concerned.

"Maurice is having issues with Tia. She's pregnant, but wants to have an abortion, and he's against it."

Loretta frowned. "He should be. That's awful. The Bible says that children are precious gifts from God. Then again, he has no business getting no girl pregnant in the first place." But the thought of being a grandmother made her smile. "What else is going on with that boy?"

"He's into that life."

Loretta balled her fist, as her blood pressure went up. "What life?" she asked irritably.

"That hooligan life." Lemar nodded. "I don't wanna go into detail, so I'd prefer if you you didn't ask."

Loretta sighed, and then decided to change the subject. All she could do was hope and pray that her son would make good choices while he was out in the street. "So, how are you and Alvina doing?" she asked, wondering if Alvina had asked Lemar to marry her yet.

"We're doing fine," he said, scratching his head.

"Just fine?" Loretta asked.

"Yeah. Why?"

"I just asked." She wanted to tell her son what the deal was, but didn't want to spoil Alvina's surprise. "Would you like for me to fix you some leftover fried chicken?" she asked, standing up.

"Sure, Ma." *It feels good to be back home,* he thought.

Just outside, a man dressed in all black peered through the tinted black windows of Lemar's Benz. As he struggled to peek inside, he prayed that at least one of the doors would be unlocked. He reached for the handle of the back door. The man silently hoped the alarm wouldn't go off. He braced himself, as he opened the door. There was no alarm.

How stupid can he be, he thought. He tossed the bag onto the back seat and closed the door. He turned away from the car and trotted off.

After spending the day with his mother, Lemar left his childhood home feeling better than ever. As he reached the end of the block, he saw a squad car coming toward him. He frowned and looked behind him, seeing another squad car pull up.

"I wonder what they want now?" he asked himself.

A chubby black police officer, with an arrogant walk, jumped out of his squad car and approached Lemar.

"Why do you keep sweating me, Officer Bailey?" Lemar asked.

"Driver's license and registration," Bailey responded, as the other officer got out the car behind him. "Search his car," Officer Bailey ordered to his partner.

Lemar laughed. "You don't have anything on me, you idiot. Besides, you should spend more time worrying about getting those braces off your teeth, with your old ass," Lemar joked. He handed Bailey his driver's license and registration, as the other officer opened the back door to his car.

Bailey ignored the comments. He was used to it. Even his co-workers joked from time to time about a man his age wearing braces. He went to call in Lemar's license, just to see if it was valid. Lemar turned on the radio and relaxed, his mind was set on going home.

Bailey returned to the car and handed Lemar his license and registration, just as Reynolds walked up with a plastic bag in hand.

"I found this," he said to Bailey.

Bailey opened the bag, reached for his flashlight, and turned it on. The light beamed into the contents of the bag. "There's at least two ounces of crack cocaine here," he said.

Lemar kept his cool. He had sense enough to know this was a set up. It wouldn't do him a bit of good to protest. *Who would do this to me?* The only person he could think of was sloppy looking Bailey, who called himself a real policeman, and who stood there with a wide grin.

Bailey smiled at Lemar. "Officer Reynolds, please cuff this low life drug-dealer."

Reynolds opened the door, as Lemar turned the engine off. He pulled Lemar out of the car, and forced him to the hood. Within seconds, he was handcuffed and placed in the back of Bailey's squad car.

Lemar took a deep breath, trying to control his anger. The only thing he wanted to do now was to get in touch with his lawyer.

When Brian came into the house from a busy day of money

making, the house was empty.

This would be the perfect time to bring a crackhead home to blow me, he thought.

He reached into his pocket, walked over to the table in the dinning room, and counted his money. He sat at the head of the table, as the smell of money made his dick hard.

Suddenly, he heard a door slam from somewhere in the apartment, which made him realize he wasn't alone.

"Tia? Ma?" Neither of them answered. Brian heard what sounded like a coin dropping on the floor. "Whose there?" he asked, as he got up from the table.

There was no answer. Brian sighed, thinking it was nothing. He sat back down at the table, never noticing the figure that tip-toed down the stairs toward him, with a revolver in his hand.

❄ ❄ ❄

Maurice stormed in the house, rushed Courtney off the phone, and immediately paged Brian. He paced around the room, leaving Courtney terrified as she looked at him.

"What's wrong, Maurice?" she asked.

He shook his head. "Nothing," he replied.

He went into the dining room and sat at the table. He fidgeted in the chair, then got back up to pace around the room again. The phone rang. Maurice answered on the first ring, hoping it was Brian. He wanted to tell Brian that someone may be after him. Although he knew Brian could take care of himself, Maurice felt he had to warn his friend.

Maurice slammed the phone and sat back down. "It was someone with the wrong damn number."

"Maurice, what's the matter?" Courtney asked again.

He banged a fist on the table. "Nothing!"

Courtney shook her head. "Nothing? It doesn't look like that to me."

Maurice got up and paced for the third time. "I'm just a bit hyped because of something that just happened."

"What happened?"

"I had to handle some fools just now," he said, sitting back down.

"What?" Courtney asked, wanting to know what he meant by that.

Maurice nodded. "I don't know if they died or not, but I tried to kill them. I know they got hit up."

Courtney walked over to him. "What do you mean, you tried to kill them? How many of them are you talking about?"

"Four." Maurice explained. He became even more restless as he told her the details.

"Maurice, please calm down." Courtney put her hand on his shoulder.

He reached in his belt strap, pulled out his 9mm, and placed it on the table. "You're right. I need to get my thoughts together."

"I'll fix you something to eat," Courtney said, looking at Maurice as he got up from the table.

He grabbed his gun, and went down to the basement.

Courtney stood over the stove, preparing her famous cabbage and beef stew. She thought about how easy it was for these young men -- or anyone -- to get in trouble. *Things shouldn't be this way,* she thought. *What's wrong with these young guys?*
At that moment, the doorbell rung, disturbing her thoughts. She hurried to the front door and opened it.

Tia stood in the entryway, dressed in blue jeans and a black long-sleeved sweatshirt. Her face had despair written all over it. Her eyes were watery, like she'd been crying.

"Tia, what's wrong?" Courtney asked.

"My brother was shot," she responded. "He's in serious condition at Holy Cross Hospital."

"Oh, Tia, I'm so sorry," Courtney said, thinking about what Maurice had just told her about somebody looking for Brian. "Do the police have any suspects?"

Tia shook her head. "No."

"Maurice is downstairs. You're welcome to go on down."

"Thanks, Courtney."

When Tia got downstairs, she saw Maurice sitting on the edge of the bed, with a gun in his hand, as he watched an old western movie.

"Hi, Maurice," she said, with hesitation.

Maurice turned to look at her, before turning his gaze back toward the television.

"Maurice, I know you're mad at me, but..."

"Don't even waste your time, Tia," he told her. "I don't want to hear anything you gotta say."

She remained quiet for a few seconds. "Maurice, you gotta listen to me."

He jumped up from the bed and walked over to her. "I stopped listening to you, when you got rid of our baby, Tia! I can't and won't forgive..."

"Maurice, shut up and listen to me!" she said, cutting him off. "Somebody shot Brian! He's in serious condition at Holy Cross Hospital. I just came here to tell you dat."

He looked at her with a straight face, his displeasure vanishing a little. "Stop playing," he said.

"Look. When my mother got home today, she found Brian lying on his side, unconscious. He was shot three times in the back, twice in the arm, and once in the back of the neck."

Maurice thought back to the shots he busted at those fools in the Chevy Blazer earlier. He wasn't crazy. He knew he had killed at least two of the four men who were inside the truck. He could only think of one explanation -- that the other two had gone to Brian's house and shot him in retaliation.

He eyed Tia, looking her up and down, paying close attention to her stomach. "Let's go to the hospital," he ordered.

❊　❊　❊

Brian lay in the hospital bed, fighting for his life. He'd been placed in ICU a short time ago. Bonita stood by his side, sobbing as Tia held her mother's hand.

Maurice looked at his friend bewildered, confused as to how those fools had time to go and shoot Brian, after he'd whipped the hell out of them with fifteen gunshots. He knew he hadn't killed all of them, but he was absolutely sure he'd left two of them slain.

Just then, a doctor came in the room, and walked over toward Brian.

"He's lost a great deal of blood. We're about to take him to surgery in a few minutes. His pulse is weak, and I'm gonna level with you all, there's a good chance that he may not make it through the night."

"You can't let him die!" Maurice yelled to the doctor.

"Son, he's suffered three gunshots to his back, two of them ruptured both of his lungs. The bullet that entered his neck, lucki-ly exited a few centimeters away from his throat. We're doing everything we can," the doctor replied.

"He's right. You can't let him die!" Bonita screamed.

The doctor turned around, and saw the readout of Brian's tem-perature. "His body temperature is dropping slowly."

At that moment, Brian opened his eyes. They rolled to the back of his head, but as weak as he was, he spoke. "Don't let me die," he whispered.

Maurice looked at him. "Brian, you're awake!"

"Don't...let...me die," Brian said again. "Maurice...it was..."

Maurice frowned. "Who? Who shot you, Brian?"

A loud beeping sound was heard, and a straight digital flat line appeared. In a fraction of a second, Brian was gone.

Tia put a hand over her mouth, as tears streamed down her face. Maurice couldn't believe what had just happened. He looked at Brian again, before leaving the room. He stopped at the large window in the hallway just outside Brian's room, listening to Bonita holler.

"Nooo!" she screamed.

Maurice heard footsteps, and turned to see a weeping Tia running toward him. She put an arm around his shoulder, and cried like there was no end. Maurice shook his head, as he fought like hell to keep from crying.

"Do you have any idea who could've done this?" he asked.

"No," Tia responded, as she continued to cry.

He frowned, looking away from the window. As a hoodlum, he thought of the most drastic thing that he could think of -- murder.

"Whoever did this is gonna die," he promised.

Tia backed away from Maurice. "Thanks. I'm sure whoever did this deserves to die." She kissed his check before going back into the room to be with her mother.

❊　❊　❊

Officer Bailey stood with Detective Sanders and Officer Reynolds at the spot where, only a few hours ago, someone had shot and killed two men inside a Chevy Blazer, wounding two others.

Young Assassin

"A young guy, between sixteen and nineteen, did this," one of the wounded men told them, before being taken to the hospital. "He was driving a convertible white Saab 900."

Sanders attention was directed to a truck that sat in the middle of the closed intersection, with shattered windows and a dent in the right fender. He looked at the other officers.

"My advice is to be on the lookout for a convertible white Saab 900 with a dent on its left side," Sanders said.

Bailey looked at him. "Right," he said suspiciously.

Chapter Twelve

Lemar had been placed in Central Cell. The environment was familiar, as he listened to the crazy conversations of other prisoners, and waited for Ryan to arrive. He was pissed off at the police for doing something so devious as planting drugs in his car. Lemar knew Officer Bailey was responsible for setting him up, so he was going to make sure the crooked cop paid with his life.

He thought back to the year before, when Bailey saw him sitting in his car outside Oak Terrace. "I'm going to help you clean up your act. One way or another," he remembered Bailey saying. It had sounded more like a threat than a warning. Now, almost a year later, Officer Bailey had finally gotten him.

Suddenly, an officer called his name and opened his cell. "Your lawyer's here."

He led Lemar up a flight of stairs to a room, where Ryan sat behind a table.

"You have twenty-five minutes," the officer said. He closed the door and locked it.

"How are you holding up?" Ryan asked.

"Fine," Lemar replied, taking a seat.

"Well, from what you've told me, I think we can make the case point out Officer Bailey as a suspect."

"The fool planted that crap in my car, Ryan! He's been watching me for years. He's the same cop who arrested my friend, Seth, a couple of years ago. Even if I get out, I know he's still gonna fuck with me."

"Officer Bailey is a dirty cop, Lemar. It's apparent he has it in for you. For an officer to plant drugs in someone's car is very low, but don't worry, we can beat this. All we have to do is declare your innocence and state your case."

"You gotta get me out of this one, Ryan. And in this case, I really am innocent."

"I know you are," Ryan replied, shaking his head. I'll start an investigation. I'm willing to bet he didn't cover his tracks very well."

"Cool. Are you ready for my brother's murder case?" he asked, knowing he might be locked up when Maurice's case went to trial.

"As ready as I'll ever be," Ryan answered. "The evidence on Maurice is pretty solid. If we do win his case, it'll be by the skin of our teeth."

Instantly, Lemar thought about Alvina. He'd been on his way home to propose to her when he was arrested. *I hope this isn't a sign not to get married*, he thought.

Ryan stood up. "Is there anything you can think of that you might need?"

"Yeah, please call my apartment and tell Alvina that I'm locked up."

"Is that it?"

Lemar nodded. "That's it."

"Okay," Ryan responded, picking up his briefcase. "I'll see you in court."

After Ryan left, Lemar got up and knocked on the door. He waited patiently, as the officer opened it, and led him back to his cell.

❋   ❋   ❋

The next morning, Maurice woke up early with Brian's murder, as well as Tia's abortion, fresh on his mind. He had lost a child and a dear friend. He felt a painful void in his heart, thinking how so much sorrow could've come to him so suddenly. He also thought about his mother, and wondered what she'd been doing since the night he stormed out of her house. He missed her terribly.

He got out of bed and stretched, with the thought of going upstairs to fix himself some breakfast. As he started up the stairs, he smelled bacon frying. He looked forward to seeing Courtney, but when he opened the door, he was surprised to see a strange, short woman with cornrows, wearing a tight body suit and five inch heels in the kitchen.

"Who the hell are you?" he asked, eyeing the woman up and down.

"I'm Courtney's friend, Rhea," the woman answered. "And you are?"

"I'm Maurice," he told her. "I've been staying here for a while until I get a place."

Maurice looked at the clock on the wall. *Damn, it's only 6:13. What is this lady doing here so early in the morning?*

"Courtney has told me a lot about you. She says you're a good kid."

"I try to be," he responded, grabbing a bag of pretzels off the refrigerator.

Rhea placed the bacon on a plate, next to a burnt waffle.

"You still in school?" she asked.

"Why? Are you the police? Cause you asking a lot of questions."

She looked at him with her mouth wide open.

"I guess not," Maurice said walking away.

He went upstairs to take a shower, wondering what this day would bring, and if Rhea would still be there when he come back down. After all, she was kinda cute, and he hadn't had sex since he and Tia broke up.

As he brushed his teeth, Bandit entered his mind for some strange reason. Maurice knew he had to kill his crew leader. Bandit had crossed the line by robbing his brother. And because of Bandit, he'd gotten abducted. *The niggah even had the nerve to accept money from Lemar to kill the dude who kidnapped me.*

Because of that, Bandit had to pay threefold. Maurice contemplated about telling the rest of his crew. They were loyal to him and Lemar, but they were also loyal to Bandit. But Maurice didn't believe for one second they would remain loyal to Bandit once they found out what he'd done — even if it was three years ago. They would gladly expel their leader, and label him a deceitful traitor. Bandit was going to get what was coming to him, and soon.

Smiling to himself, Maurice went downstairs. He frowned, as he saw Courtney and Rhea tongue-kissing one another on the sofa. He had to rub his eyes to convince himself that they weren't deceiving him. Courtney and Rhea broke from their embrace, when they saw Maurice looking at them.

"Maurice!" Courtney said shocked. "I didn't know you were here."

"Pretend like I'm not," he told them and hurried back upstairs.

By the time he left for school, Courtney and her friend were gone. He locked the front door, and walked toward his car.

When Maurice reached his Saab, he got in, let the top down, and pulled off. His mind raced as he drove down the block. He smiled, as he thought about the day when he bought the Saab from Brian. *Boy, that was a happy day for both of us*, he thought. As he continued to drive, his smile turned into a frown when he wondered if Lemar was able to pay off Veronica Russell. He didn't see the cop sitting in the squad car, who'd been watching the car for sometime. Maurice was a block away from school when the cop pulled him over. He frowned, wondering what he wanted.

The officer walked to his side of the car, as Maurice rolled down the window, prepared to hand over his driver's license.

"My name's Officer Brown, sir. I need for you to come down to the Fourth District."

Maurice smirked. "For what? I'm minding my business."

Officer Brown looked at him, feeling he owed the young man an explanation. "A double homicide occurred yesterday evening near Aspen Road, and a vehicle like this one was sighted at the shooting. Please step out of the car and come with me."

"Why?" Maurice asked.

"Because, you're under arrest."

Maurice turned off the engine and stepped out of the car. Officer Brown cuffed Maurice, and pushed him into the back of the squad car. As the squad car pulled away, Maurice thought, *I wonder who could've possibly seen me pop those idiots in that truck yesterday?*

When he arrived at the precinct, a female officer escorted him into a room full of men. They all were ordered to stand up against the wall, and to face forward. Maurice shook his head, as he stared at the dark glass in front of his face. *I can't believe I'm in a fucking lineup*, he thought. Maurice had sense enough to know there was a witness on the other side, trying to provide a positive ID of the person who'd fatally shot the two men, to the police. He just hoped it wasn't one of the dude's who'd survived.

As suspected, one of the two men who'd lived after the ambush was on the other side of the glass, looking at the five possible suspects. Officer Reynolds stood next to him. "Just take your time," he said.

Just then, Officer Brown came in the room, with a cup of coffee in his hand. "Do you recognize any of these men as the man who shot at you and your friends?"

There was a brief moment of silence before he answered.

"No, I don't see him."

The witness focused his eyes on the young man in the center dressed in an Asics T-shirt and jeans.

"Are you sure?" Reynolds asked. "Look at them again." Reynolds eyes revealed dark circles, as he if had no sleep, and desperately needed a drink.

After another few seconds of silence, the witness responded, "None of these guys look familiar."

"Are you sure you know what he looks like?" Brown asked. He noticed the witness looking at one of the guys strangely.

"Yeah, but I don't see him."

"The guy in the center, are you sure it wasn't him?"

"Yeah, I'm sure."

Reynolds let out a huge sigh. "Okay then. I guess you can leave. We'll get an officer to take you back to the hospital."

"Okay, thank you." The man left, leaving Brown and Reynolds in the room alone.

Thirty minutes later, the charges against Maurice were dropped. He smiled, as he strutted out of the police station a guilty, but free man.

❋　❋　❋

Veronica Russell was at home preparing for school when the phone rang.

"Hello?" she answered.

"This Veronica?" a masculine voice asked.

"Yes, this is Veronica. Who's this?"

"If you testify, your mother dies, and then you're next, bitch!"

Veronica felt a deep fear in her heart. "Who is this?" she asked nervously.

There was silence, then laughter. "If you testify, your mother gets pumped in her ass with a twelve-gauge slug."

Veronica slammed the phone down, and called the police. Although afraid, she still managed to make it to school.

She could barely stop shaking, as she walked into her class. Veronica never thought she'd be intimidated the way she'd just been. But the caller had struck so much fear in her heart that she was thinking of not testifying. Besides, her life along with her mother's, was at risk. *Why did I get myself into this? I should've kept my mouth shut like everyone else.*

Veronica was a senior, and instantly began to think about her long-awaited graduation. She knew if she went to court to testify, something terrible would come out of it, but if she lied, she could be locked up for perjury. Veronica was stuck between a rock and a hard place.

She got up and walked out of her French class after the first-period bell sounded. Walking down a hall flooded with students, she felt the firm touch of a hand on her arm, and then felt something cold strike her stomach. Veronica dropped her books and fell to the floor, as students quickly walked by.

A teacher happened to see the painful look on her face from a distance, and the fresh bloodstains coming through her shirt. The teacher immediately rushed to her side.

"Are you okay?" he asked.

"No, someone just stabbed me," she whispered.

He looked at the flow of blood that slowly leaked from her body. As a student walked past, he grabbed the student by the arm.

"Hey, you! Run down to the main office and have someone call 911! Hurry!"

The student, a lanky light-skinned boy with freckles, looked down at Veronica, and ran as fast as he could to the office.

Young Assassin

❖   ❖   ❖

Maurice sat in his guidance counselor's office. He and several other senior students were trying to determine the amount of credits they needed in order to graduate, when there was a knock on the door.

"Come in," the guidance counselor said.

The door opened, and four D.C. police officers came in with their guns drawn. "I'm Officer Charles Reynolds. The principal told me that a student by the name of Maurice Patterson was here."

Maurice shook his head. *Now what*, he wondered.

"He's right there," the counselor pointed.

Maurice remained calm as two of the policemen approached him.

"What did I do?" he asked, putting his pencil down.

"Maurice, you're a suspect for the attempted murder of Veronica Russell," one officer said.

"I didn't attempt to murder anybody," Maurice told him.

The guidance counselor stood up. "When did this occur?" she asked Officer Reynolds.

"Approximately forty minutes ago," he told her.

"Maurice has been in my office waiting to speak with me for over an hour."

"Are you absolutely sure?" Reynolds asked.

"I'm positive," she said, smelling the alcohol from Reynolds's breath.

"And he hasn't left this room within that time?"

"He's been here the whole time," one of the students added.

Reynolds looked at Maurice long and hard. "Bring him in for questioning anyway," he ordered.

Maurice was taken to the Fourth District Precinct for the

second time. He held his head down, as he walked down the hall, accompanied by four policemen. After catching the elevator to the bottom level, he was led to an office.

"Have a seat," Officer Reynolds said. "So, Maurice, if you didn't stab Veronica Russell, can you tell me who did?" Reynolds asked, sitting across from him.

Maurice looked at him. "I don't know who stabbed her," he said calmly. "As a matter of fact, I don't even know who she is."

"Well, I think you do," Reynolds replied. "You see, she's supposed to testify against your ass in court. She also called here this morning, and informed us about a threatening phone call she received from someone who told her not to testify. You wouldn't happen to know anything about that, would you?"

"No, I wouldn't," Maurice responded.

"Do you know how severe the penalty is for terrorizing a government witness?"

"Why should I care?" Maurice asked. "I didn't do anything."

"And you don't have any idea who called her on the phone and threatened her?"

"No."

"Well, whoever did that is probably the same asshole who stabbed her today," Reynolds said, with a evil look on his face.

Maurice got up from the chair unbothered. "Can I go now?"

"You know, Maurice, I saw you here the morning after you were arrested for a double homicide."

"So?"

"So, I see you have a habit of being charged with murders. I suggest for your own sake, you stay out of trouble, since trouble has a way of finding you."

"I'm not interested in your advice. If you're not gonna charge me, then let me go."

Reynolds locked his eyes with Maurice for a few seconds, then looked over at the man sitting behind the table. "Detective

Young Assassin

Sanders, could you please escort Mr. Patterson out of here, before I beat the shit out of him!"

Chapter Thirteen

Maurice sat at the table on the far left of the courtroom, looking at the twelve jurors, while his attorney, Ryan Dalby, sat next to him. A part of Maurice was happy that the case was finally being tried. Months had passed and the stress of possibly being convicted was starting to wear him down. The courtroom was silent as the prosecution team waited for their star witness to arrive.

Twenty minutes had passed since Maurice had taken the stand, answering questions from the prosecution and the defense. Without Veronica Russell's testimony, the prosecution didn't have much of a case. Other people who were rumored to have witnessed the homicide outside of the deli that day, had been urged to come forward, but never did.

"Your Honor, the prosecution's witness is a no show," Ryan said, standing up.

"The witness will report to court," the prosecuting attorney, Joshua Weinberg, replied.

"Well, the witness better hurry up!" the impatient judge said. "This Court is already behind schedule."

Twenty more minutes passed. As Maurice fidgeted in his chair, the judge sighed. "Counselors, approach the bench, please," he ordered. Both Weinberg and Ryan walked toward the front of the court.

"Please give it more time," urged Weinberg.

"Counselor, enough time has been given," the judge said. "No more time can be wasted. Your witness either has cold feet, or didn't remember she had a court date. I don't know which one it is, but the defendant's testimony is all I've heard, and will be considered the truth by me."

"But..."

"I'm prepared to make my ruling. Now, both of you step back," the judge ordered.

Ryan turned and gave Maurice a thumbs-up and smiled.

※　※　※

Maurice walked into the familiar household for the first time in months. He smiled, as he saw his mother looking at him from the sofa.

"Hi, Ma. How you been?"

"Maurice, how did you get in here?" Loretta asked standing up.

"How many times have I told you to stop leaving the front door unlocked? You don't live in Georgetown," Maurice said, walking toward his mother.

"It's good to see you, son," Loretta said, hugging him tightly. "Have you been to see Lemar?" she asked.

"No, but his court date is next week."

Maurice wanted to tell her about the outcome of his own day in court, but remained silent. It was important not to mess up the moment by saying the wrong thing, or getting on the wrong subject, as he sought to renew his bond with the woman who had raised him.

"Ma, I'm ready to come back home," he blurted out.

"I'm ready for you to come back, too. But first we have to talk."

"Ma, I'm sorry I've disappointed you," Maurice replied, reading his mother's mind.

"Maurice, I'm not going to tolerate a hoodlum living under my roof," Loretta replied. "As you know, I threw your brother out for that mess, and threw your ass out too. I'll let you come back, but understand this. If you mess up again, I won't hesitate to throw you out again. Do I make myself clear?"

"Loud and clear." For a moment there was silence, except for the running water, coming from upstairs. "Who else is here?" Maurice asked.

"I have a surprise for you. You'll see who it is soon."

Loretta knew that God would answer her prayers for her son to come back home. It seemed as though every time she put her trust and faith in Him, He delivered.

"Maurice, how's school coming?"

"Good, it's almost over."

"Are you graduating?"

"I think so."

"You think?"

"Yeah, this year has been tough," he said, realizing the running water had stopped. "I hope to make you proud."

"What kind of grades have you been getting?" Loretta asked.

"I'm not gonna lie to you, Ma. I'm a C student now."

Loretta was disappointed. Both of her sons had always been straight A students. "So, you're just getting by?"

"It's not like I'm failing. You didn't get on Lemar's case after he dropped out of college a few years ago."

"Lemar was grown, and not living in my house. You, on the other hand, aren't grown, and now want to come back under my roof. But that can always change, you know."

Maurice looked at the seriousness on Loretta's face and nodded. "I understand," he said.

"So, I'm going to ask you again, son. Will you be graduating from high school?"

"Yes, Ma'am."

Loretta decided to change the subject. She didn't want to argue with her son on his first day back. "I heard about your friend, Brian."

"I'd like to know who killed him," he said, with his head down. "And even more importantly, why they did it?"

"It just doesn't make sense how these young men are being shot and killed all the time," she commented. "And what's this I hear about you living a hooligan's life?"

Before he could answer, he heard footsteps upstairs. Suddenly, he saw someone in a pair of black slippers and a paisley robe slowly coming down the stairs. When the person was finally in full view, he frowned. It was Leonard Patterson, Maurice's long-lost father. The man who had cradled him as a baby, spanked him as a child whenever he did something bad, gave him a dollar whenever he did something good, and told him bedtime stories after tucking him in at night.

"Hello, Maurice," Leonard said. "It's been a long time." He smiled happily.

"Why is he here, and dressed in a bathrobe?" Maurice asked his mother angrily.

"Because I live here," Leonard responded. "Your mother and I have patched things up."

"What do you mean, patched things up?" Maurice asked, with a blank expression on his face. His eyes moved back and forth between both of his parents.

"Maurice, your father and me have..."

Leonard held up a hand. "Loretta, let me tell him."

"Tell me what?" Maurice asked.

"Maurice, your mother and I were remarried a few weeks ago."

Maurice looked from Leonard to Loretta and smiled, then turned around. He looked back at them, as he headed for the door.

"Where are you going?" Loretta asked.

"I need some time alone Ma. I'll be back later."

And with that, he opened the front door and hurried out.

❖   ❖   ❖

Troy jogged from the Avenue to the playground on Tilden Place, as night fell. Something was eating away at him, and he had to get in touch with Maurice to tell him about it.

He reached the basketball court, and saw a few guys shooting hoops. He walked into the rec center, and when he saw that the director wasn't around, he picked up the phone and dialed a number. A feminine voice answered on the second ring.

"Hello."

"Hi, Courtney, is Maurice home?"

"No, I think he's at his mother's house," she replied. "He told me he was going back home."

"Okay, thanks," Troy said.

He hung up and dialed Maurice's mother's number. The phone rang six times before it was answered.

"Hello?" Maurice said.

"Maurice, I got something to tell you, but not over the phone, man. Meet me at the playground as soon as you can."

"All right, I'll be there in a minute," Maurice responded.

Troy was on the basketball court playing a one-on-one against somebody, when Maurice arrived. He gave the ball to the guy he was playing against and walked toward his friend.

"Man, I got some news to tell you," Troy said.

"Good or bad?" Maurice asked.

Troy looked at him. "Bad. Real bad."

"What's up? We gotta go handle some fools or something?"

Young Assassin

Troy gestured for Maurice to follow him off the court. He didn't want anyone to hear their conversation. "Were you aware that Lemar was set up?"

"Set up?"

"Yeah. Officer Bailey found a few ounces of crack in your brother's car when he pulled him over and arrested him. Lemar knows Bailey put it there."

"He never told me anything about being set up."

"Because he probably didn't want your crazy ass to go out and kill anybody."

Maurice looked at Troy. "Who told you this?"

"Seth. He wrote me a letter. Your brother is who told him."

Maurice clenched his fist as anger swelled up inside him. "I should kill that petty ass cop!"

"Bailey's gone too far this time," Troy commented. "He's operating far above the law. You should separate him from that badge real soon."

"Well, if my brother receives any time, Bailey might as well cancel Christmas," Maurice replied.

Chapter Fourteen

Lemar, dressed in a black leather suit, stood alongside Maurice on the porch of their mother's house, looking up and down the block, as the cloudy sky showed signs of rain. The drug possession charges against Lemar had been dropped because of the lack of evidence. Ryan Dalby was preparing to file suit against the D.C.P.D. in his defense.

Alvina stepped outside the house and joined them. "Maurice, can I have a private word with Lemar?"

"You sure can. Talk to you later, bro." Maurice gave Lemar a pound before going into the house.

"It's good to see you out of those prison clothes," Alvina said, moving closer. She kissed his cheek and put her head on his shoulder.

"It's nice to be out of prison clothes," Lemar responded.

He rested his chin on the top of her head. After staying in that position for a few minutes, Alvina lifted her head and quickly stepped away. She folded her arms and turned away. After taking a deep breath, she turned back around to face him.

"So, where do you go from here?" she asked.

"What do you mean?"

"Lemar, I want you to leave that flamboyant hustler lifestyle in the past," she said, her voice soft and tender. "I want you to move on. You have enough money and enough stability." She took his hand and squeezed it. "Don't allow yourself to be controlled by desire. Go back to college and get your degree. It's time you start making better choices, Lemar. Do it for the sake of our future."

He took a deep breath and looked into her eyes. "I couldn't agree with you more."

"It's time for you to get your life together," she said. "No, it's past that time. You're twenty-three years old, sweetheart. It's time to get serious. If you continue to do the wrong thing, Lemar, you're putting us both at risk."

"And what does the future hold for us?" he asked.

"Either happiness or unhappiness," Alvina said to him softly. "Guaranteed happiness, if you abandon the way that leads to unhappiness."

"It's good to know you really care about me," he said, kissing her forehead twice. "I love you."

Alvina wondered if he thought she was after his money. In fact, she appreciated Lemar for who he was, and not for what he was. She just wanted him to give up the hustler mentality. But for some reason, she'd always been too afraid to tell him how she felt about his line of work — if one could call it that.

"I'm gonna quit dealing." Lemar blurted out.

Alvina smiled. *Did I hear him correctly? Is he really going to quit?*

Lemar continued. "I've brought too much attention to myself, and the cops are gonna be stalking me, waiting for me to slip up." He pulled her close to him. "So, I'm gonna quit and do something more constructive and positive with my life."

She smiled and hugged him as tightly as she possibly could. "I love you."

"I love you more," he replied.

Just then, a squad car rode slowly down the street and stopped in front of the house. Lemar stared angrily, as Officers Bailey and Reynolds got out the car and stepped onto the sidewalk.

by Mike G

"So, I see you beat that drug rap, huh, Patterson?" Officer Bailey asked.

At that moment, Loretta and Leonard came outside. Loretta looked at the two officers. "May I help you?" she asked.

"They were just leaving, Ma," Lemar said.

"We're on to you, Patterson," Bailey remarked. "We'll be watching every single move you make, punk."

Maurice appeared in the doorway and focused on Officer Reynolds. He kept quiet, hoping the cop wouldn't notice him.

"You shouldn't worry about me, officer," Lemar said coldly. "You should be more worried about those manufacturing evidence and trespassing charges I'm pressing against you." Lemar laughed. "You're finished."

"Good luck trying to prove that punk," Bailey replied.

"Leave him alone! Go arrest some real criminals!" Loretta yelled.

She felt Leonard's hands on her shoulders, trying to reduce the tension that was building up.

Maurice kept his eyes on Reynolds, wondering if he should turn around to avoid being seen. But it was too late, he'd caught Reynolds' attention

"Maurice Patterson. Did you kill anybody today?" Reynolds asked.

"Go back in the house, Maurice," Lemar said, in a commanding voice.

Maurice nodded, looking back at the officers, as he turned around and went back inside.

"I'm not going to ask you again," Loretta said. "Leave."

Lemar let go of Alvina and walked down the steps. "You got some beef with me, Mister Officer?" He spread his arms wide. "You want me? Well, here I am. Come and get me."

Bailey looked at him and smiled. Then looked at the people on the porch, as he turned and walked back to his squad car.

Reynolds gave a mocking salute before getting in the car. Bailey ignited the engine and pulled off.

Lemar shook his head, the displeasure he felt leaving him as he watched the squad car go down the street. Suddenly Alvina was there, stroking the back of his neck, offering comfort.

Leonard looked at them. "You okay, Lemar?"

"Yes, sir," he said, as a corrupt thought crossed his mind.

Leonard and Loretta went back into the house, leaving the couple outside.

"Where were we?" Lemar asked.

"See, that's the nonsense I'm talking about. Aren't you tired of that?" Alvina said, crossing her arms.

"Yeah, I am. But don't worry. I'm getting out the game."

Alvina smiled. "We left off with saying how much we love each other. But more importantly, I was trying to tell you that I wanna marry you."

Lemar was shocked. He had no idea that Alvina felt that way. "I wanna marry you too."

"So, when are we gonna announce our engagement?" Alvina asked excitedly.

"Let's do it at dinner tonight," he said. "But first I have something to discuss with my brother."

Maurice was lying flat on his back in the middle of his bedroom floor, doing a set of crunches when Lemar walked in. Lemar smiled, as he looked around the room, at the brilliant drawings on the wall. He walked over to Maurice's dresser and came across a disturbing piece of paper.

"When did Brian die?" Lemar asked.

"The day you were arrested."

Lemar looked at Brian's picture. "Damn." He scanned the obituary, before putting it back on the dresser.

Maurice got up and faced his brother, who'd taken a seat on the edge of his bed.

"So, what's up?"

"I'm about to quit hustling."

Maurice looked at him and smirked. "Yeah, right."

"I'm not joking. That was a close call with Bailey, and it convinced me that it's time to move on."

Maurice crossed his arms. "Move on to what?"

"I don't know yet, but I'm thinking about opening a clothing store. I'm not sure what I'm gonna do, but hustling is definitely out."

"You gonna let Bailey scare you?"

"Look, that was a sign for me to get the hell outta this game."

Maurice remained silent, as a thoughtful expression appeared on his face. "Just like that?"

"I can't risk jail time, or my future with Alvina. She means too much to me. Plus, Ryan will see to it that a jury convicts Bailey."

Maurice thought about the conversation he'd just had with Troy about killing Bailey. *I've already killed one cop, so killing another one is just putting in work.*

"Bailey is as good as dead," Maurice said, looking into his brother's fearful gaze. He looked in the mirror and rubbed his fade before leaving. "I'm out, bro."

Damn, that conversation didn't go the way I wanted it to, Lemar thought.

Maurice walked down Kalhoun Avenue in all black, along with a 9mm that he'd spray-painted black, tucked in the lightweight boots he had on.

The wind blew as he took the gun out of his boot and

removed the safety catch. He looked in all directions, seeing no one nearby. He reached into his back pocket and patted until he felt his other clip. He smiled, and walked a few blocks to where Troy was waiting on the corner.

"He's been hard to spot so far," Troy said, looking at Maurice. "I've only seen a few police cars go down the Avenue since I've been out here."

"We might be in the wrong spot," Maurice responded. "We might want to walk."

Troy reached into the pocket of his L.L. Bean jacket for a blunt and a lighter, as they walked in the direction of Seventh and Kalhoun. Maurice smiled at Troy's boldness, as he smoked the gunja out in the open. By the time they reached Eighth Street, Troy spotted a youngster being patted down, by no other than Officer Bailey.

"There he is!" Troy shouted, with his finger pointed in Bailey's direction. "Go into that alley and wait for me to lure him to you."

Officer Bailey usually didn't work double shifts, but when his replacement called in sick just before he was to get off, he didn't mind working more hours. He'd patrolled around the whole city before coming back Uptown.

As he searched the youngster, thoughts about Lemar entered his mind. He knew the young drug-dealer hated him with a burning passion, but he could care less. He was determined to stop Lemar from helping flood drugs in the Uptown neighborhoods.

He thought about what Lemar had told him: *You should be worried about the manufacturing evidence and trespassing charges I'm pressing against you. You're finished.*

Bailey's thoughts disappeared when he wasn't able to find narcotics on the boy. "Get out of here!" Bailey shouted, as he jammed his nightstick into the boy's throat. "If I see you out here again, I'm gonna lock your ass up!"

The boy looked at Bailey and nodded tearfully, as he walked away quietly. Bailey looked at the young man with an evil stare until he was out of sight. Suddenly, he smelled the aroma of weed blowing by him. When he looked around, he saw a young man standing by the hood of his patrol car, smoking a blunt.

"Why don't you pick on somebody your own size?" Troy asked, with a smile on his face.

"You've got balls, you know that?" Bailey said.

Troy smiled, and flipped the blunt onto the hood of Bailey's squad car.

Tightening the grip on his baton, Bailey stormed after Troy, who'd already turned and walked away quickly.

Bailey followed him into a nearby alley, and saw Troy rolling up another blunt. He smiled, turned, and kept walking.

At that moment, Bailey thought he saw a silhouette just ahead, as he Troy spat in his direction and ran down the alley.

"Come here you little punk!" Bailey shouted, and ran after him.

As Troy hopped over a few fences, Bailey heard something hit the ground. He turned and looked down the alley. Straining his eyes, he saw a dark figure standing a few feet away. Bailey watched as the figure came closer. Just as he reached for his gun, he was hit by an onslaught of bullets. He fell to the ground, face down and screamed out in pain.

"I'm a cop!" he cried out to the shooter. "Do you know who you're fucking with?"

Bailey managed to pull his gun from his holster, but the figure came charging at him, and kicked the weapon from his hand, making it slide down the alley.

"Are you fucking crazy?" Bailey asked.

"Die, niggah!" Maurice said. He aimed his weapon to the side of Bailey's head, and squeezed the trigger repeatedly until the clip was empty.

Maurice jogged toward the playground, and saw Troy standing in the middle of the basketball court, puffing on another fat blunt.

"He dead?" Troy asked.

"Shh," Maurice said, looking around to see if anyone was around.

"Ain't nobody out here, man," Troy assured him. "Did you kill his ass?"

"That motherfucka's brains got cooked like five strips of bacon," Maurice replied.

"So, Bailey fell for the trap?"

"Yeah. Thanks for setting him up for me. So, what you gonna do tonight?" Maurice asked nonchalantly.

Troy smiled. "After me and Bandit rob some fools, we gonna go find a couple of hoes to give us head."

Just then three squad cars raced down the street, followed by an ambulance.

"What you gonna do tonight?" Troy asked.

"Me and Lemar gonna hang out tonight. It's been awhile since we've done that."

"That's what's up. I'll catch you later," Troy said, giving Maurice a pound.

Maurice walked toward his house, while Troy walked to the Avenue. They both saw the bright blazing light from a D.C.P.D. chopper flying in the air, bathing the entire neighborhood.

Officer Brown raced to the scene of the crime. When he heard the badge number of the slain officer announced over the radio, he couldn't believe it. Brown walked into the alley, took a deep breath, and ducked under the yellow tape.

He walked over to the paramedics and officers standing around, to get any updates. After receiving confirmation that Bailey was really gone, he looked down at the white sheet covering the officer's body. His hands shook, as he pulled the sheet down.

by Mike G

There was a great deal of blood on the ground by his shoulder and head, and brain tissue hung out the side of his head. Brown closed his eyes and covered Bailey's body back up. An officer walked up behind him as he stood up.

"No leads on a possible killer?" Brown asked.

"I'm afraid not, my friend," Officer Olson answered.

"No witnesses?" Brown asked.

"No sir," Olson said. "People said they heard gunfire, but that's all."

Brown bit his lip. "This is the second cop killed from this district, and nobody saw anything?" He looked down and saw bullet shells lying on the ground.

"You think Lemar Patterson knows anything about this?" Olson asked. "He had every motive to kill Bailey. Or what about his wild ass brother, Maurice? After all, he does have a reputation for violence."

"I have the slightest idea, Olson," Brown answered.

Both of them looked on as the paramedics put Bailey in a body bag. Brown knew that Bailey had made a lot of enemies on the streets. It could've been anyone who shot his comrade to death.

"Olson, it's gonna be hard to sleep tonight," Officer Brown said, as he gazed up at the little bit of stars left in the sky.

Young Assassin

Chapter Fifteen

Maurice paced the streets, still on the lookout for Bandit, who was finally back in town from his routine trip to New York. With the warm temperature making him thirsty, he decided to walk to the store to get a soda. He walked two blocks to the market, and saw Troy standing by the curb with a forty-ounce of malt liquor in his hand.

"What's up, Troy?" Maurice asked.

Troy turned around. "Nothin'. What's up with you?"

"A lot of things." Maurice said, trying to sound worried.

"Like what?"

"Like Bandit," Maurice replied.

Troy grinned. "Who has that fool killed now?"

"Nobody that I know of," Maurice said, looking away. "But there's somebody after him."

"For real?" Troy looked at him. "Who is it?"

"Me," Maurice said. He lifted his shirt and showed off the Uzi on his hip.

Troy couldn't believe what he'd just heard. "Why you gonna kill him? He's our boy, ain't he?"

"Nah, and he never was," Maurice said.

Maurice told Troy what Bandit had done a few years back, and how he was involved in his kidnapping. After listening, Troy was even more shocked. He couldn't believe that Bandit had betrayed his boys.

"Do what you gotta do," Troy said.

Maurice looked over his shoulder and saw Bandit walking

across the street. "Speak of the devil," he said, pointing to Bandit.

"You about to go after him right now?" Troy asked, as his eyes widened.

"Nah, I'll get that niggah in due time," Maurice said, still watching Bandit. "I'll meet you at your house in a couple hours."

❄ ❄ ❄

J.B. looked out at Milburn Street behind his dark shades, as he sat on his porch, thinking about his future. He'd just served two hundred and nine days in jail on a drug charge.

Having to appear before a grand jury, and testify against the deceased Officer Bailey, caused him to think about leaving the fast lifestyle alone.

The smell of the roses his mother had grown in the front yard was pleasurable. Every time he took a sniff, J.B. smiled as he thought about all he had to be thankful for. He'd gotten a second chance, and wasn't gonna let the opportunity slip away.

He looked three doors down and saw Maurice step outside on the porch topless, wearing gray sweatpants. "Hey, Maurice!" he yelled.

Maurice turned and looked at J.B. "What's up, man?" He walked off his porch, cut across his neighbor's yard, and sat on the iron railing in front of J.B.'s house.

"Man, I'm gettin' out of this life. It ain't worth it," J.B. said bluntly.

Maurice smiled. "I guess you gotta do what you gotta do."

"It's time for me to learn from the past and get on wit' my life."

"So, you cutting your crew loose?" Maurice questioned.

"Why would you ask me something like that?" J.B. asked. "I'm still gonna fuck wit' you and Troy, man. I just can't live that type of life no more. Being locked up has taught me a lot. You understand, don't you?"

"Sure." Maurice replied.

"Selling drugs, carrying guns, and running from the police ain't where it's at," J.B. said.

"What are your plans now?" Maurice asked.

"I don't know," J.B. said, in a low voice. "I'm not sure. How long are you gonna continue to pop off at people?" J.B. looked at Maurice, with a serious expression.

"J.B., I can't let my guard down just yet." He looked away. "Probably ever."

"Why? All it's gonna do is lead to more violence, death or incarceration," J.B. told him, a slight frown appearing on his face.

"It's in my blood," Maurice said.

"I remember when you were a scared and shy type of dude." Maurice said proudly, "Well, that was then, and this is now."

"Okay, man, I'll holla at you later," J.B. said, turning to go inside his house.

Maurice stood on his porch alone, looking at his sporty new 300ZX that was parked and covered with a leather car cover. He felt a little stupid for spending all his money on the car.

Suddenly, Maurice saw a dirty white Chevy Camaro pulling in front of his house. He smiled, as a small petite woman with large breasts emerged from the car.

"Hey Boo," the woman said.

"You need to wash that filthy ass car, Pam," Maurice responded, as he walked back to his house.

"Shut up! I didn't come over here for you to inspect my car." Pam stood with her hands on her hips. "Are you ready to fuck or what? I don't have all day."

Young Assassin

Pam was an older hustler from the neighborhood that everyone respected because she didn't take shit from anyone. On top of that, she had three sons in prison that would send orders to kill anyone who even breathed on their mother wrong. Maurice often bought his supply of coke from Pam, which is how their love affair started.

"I'm more than ready," Maurice replied, as he opened the door.

"Is your mother home? I don't wanna get into it with her like the last time."

Maurice ignored Pam's question and led her to the basement. He didn't waste anytime taking off his clothes once they became face to face. Pam panties became moist as she looked at Maurice's smooth chest and baby six pack. *Damn, he must be working out*, she thought. Pam threw her purse on the floor, and began to undress.

"Your body looks so good for an old head," Maurice said, looking at her perfect 36C breasts.

"Boy, don't mess up the mood," Pam replied as she walked to the sofa. "Now get over here!"

Maurice followed her orders, and cupped both of her breasts in his hands, squeezing them before he climbed on top of her and penetrated her calmly. She slapped him on the ass, and pulled him closer.

"Fuck me young boy!" Pam yelled as she bit down on her lip.

Maurice smiled and did as she commanded. With each stroke he pushed his dick deeper. The pure wetness from her treasure excited him as the pace quickened. She was tight, and he loved it.

"That's it," she told him. ""Fuck me just like that."

"Okay," he replied, breathing in her face as he used all his strength to pound her harder.

Although Pam was half a decade older than him, she never let that stop her from giving him some coochie. She'd even cheated on a last boyfriend with Maurice because she just couldn't get enough.

"Does it feel good?" Maurice asked.

"Yes! Yes!"

She hugged his body with her short, toned legs, and that excited him even more as she began to scream. Everything stopped when Maurice told her he was about to cum, and immediately pulled out. Juices flew everywhere as Maurice stroked his dick to release every ounce. They both slid on the floor and sat shoulder to shoulder in exhaustion.

Ten minutes later, Pam stood up quickly put back on her clothes. She reached into her MCM bag and tossed Maurice an ounce of coke. He looked at it carefully, reached under the sofa and pulled a pistol.

"That will make you close to a G," she said.

"And this is for anybody who wants to stop me from making diit," Maurice replied, holding up his 9mm.

Pam shook her head. "I gotta go. Call me later to let me know when we can do this again." She kissed him on the forehead and headed up the stairs.

Just then, Maurice's pager beeped. He pulled it from his pocket, and noticed that Troy had beeped him. He went inside, picked the phone up and dialed the number.

"Hello."

"Troy, what's up?" he asked.

"We're goin' to The Mojito Ballroom to see the Inner City Groovers," Troy said. "You coming?"

"Nah, I'ma chill tonight," Maurice told him. "I'll probably see you sometime tomorrow."

"Cool," Troy said. "Catch you on the rebound then." He hung up the phone.

Later that night, Troy arrived at The Mojito Ballroom. From the outside, the club looked small with its red paved structure, which stood maybe twenty-nine or thirty feet tall. It had very dark brown doors on the outside. Its address, written in large black numbers, were on a rectangular glass window just above the doors.

Troy parked his car around the corner, where a long line of young people waited to go inside the club. He met up with a guy named Keith, that he and Maurice hung with every now and then from across town. They respected Keith because he was a rare type of thug, who would rob someone of their coke, then try and sell it back to them the same night.

"What's up?" a familiar voice said, when they got in line.

Both Troy and Keith looked behind them and saw Bandit, dressed in a blue tank top, Bugle Boy shorts, and black tennis shoes.

Troy smiled as Bandit approached them, while Keith thought Bandit seemed a little suspicious. He'd been taught not to trust anybody.

"What's been goin' on?" Troy asked Bandit.

"Nothing," Bandit said. "What's up with you?"

"Nothing much," Troy responded, as a smile spread across his lips. "Just hangin' out with my man, Keith."

Bandit stood behind them in line. "Where's Maurice?"

"You know this type of thing ain't his style."

They remained quiet as they waited to go inside the club. A few minutes later, two guys walked up behind them with a young woman in the middle. Troy turned around and looked at the girl, who had on a short mini skirt and red shirt. He looked at her and the guys she was with.

"Hey, Tia," Troy spoke.

Tia smiled. "Hey, Troy."

One of the guys she was with grabbed her by the arm. "You with me, girl! Stop talking to every niggah you see!"

Just then Bandit and Keith turned around.

"Joe, get your hands off me," she ordered. She looked at Troy. "This is my boyfriend, Joe."

Troy looked at the guy, and then looked her up and down. "I see you're a little fat in the front."

"I'm six months pregnant," Tia said.

"Bitches ain't shit," Troy responded. "You killed Maurice's baby, but now you gonna go out and have a kid by somebody else."

"Who you talking to, niggah?" Joe asked, stepping up to Troy. "You got some type of problem?"

Troy immediately hit Joe with a wicked left hook that made him stumble, as Keith reached for his gun. The other guy with him charged at Troy and tackled him. Bandit started stomping the dude, as Keith put his gun to Joe's head.

"Get off him before I blow your boy's brains out, niggah!" Keith shouted. The people who stood in line looked at the scene in fear.

The dude got off Troy, as Keith kept the gun against Joe's head. He finally removed the gun and put it back in his pocket.

Joe looked at them and walked down the sidewalk. "Y'all punk ass niggahs better not be here when I get back," he threatened.

Tia ran after him, along with the other guy.

"We'll be here, motherfucka!" Troy shouted. He pulled his revolver and was about to follow them, but felt a hand on his arm. He turned to look at Bandit.

"Get in touch with Maurice, and tell him to come up here with some more fire power," Bandit said, reaching for his own firearm.

❊   ❊   ❊

Young Assassin

Maurice was sitting on the sofa looking at television, then his pager beeped. He grabbed it and looked at the number, which he didn't recognize. He reached for the phone and dialed the number.

"Somebody page me?" Maurice asked, wondering if it was some crackhead who wanted to get served.

"It's Troy, Maurice. Look, me, Keith and Bandit are down at The Mojito Ballroom. And we just had a run-in with this dude, who talking big shit about coming back up here with some conflict."

"Stay right where you are," Maurice said. "I'll be right there."

"Maurice, bring two pieces," Troy said, before hanging up.

Maurice got to The Mojito Ballroom in record time. He spotted Troy and Bandit standing by a set of pay phones. He pulled up to where they were, and grabbed his 10mm and .380. Stepping out his car, he looked at his surroundings, watching for any signs of a surprise attack.

"What's up?" Maurice asked, as he walked over to his buddies. He put the .380 in his pocket, along with the clips.

"Maurice, listen to me!" Troy said. "Tia was with the dude who I told you about over the phone, and guess what?"

"What?"

"She's seven months pregnant with that niggah's baby."

Maurice eyes widened. "What?"

"He ain't playin'," Bandit added. "Her stomach's big as shit."

Maurice squeezed the handle of his 10mm as hard as he could.

Just as Troy stopped talking, an old Pontiac Trans Am came speeding from around the corner and stopped in front of the club. Five dudes stepped out the car armed.

"There they go," Bandit said.

Maurice reached in his waist and gave Troy the 9mm. He walked out in the middle of the street like the Terminator, removing the safety catch from his own weapon.

Bandit ran out in front of him and instantly started shooting. Troy's gunshots followed, then Keith, then Maurice. The line outside the club broke up and people began to scatter, screaming at the top of their lungs, terrified at the sound of the sudden gunfire.

Joe, and two others with him, turned around and started firing shots, as the two other men slithered back to the Trans Am. Maurice spotted the Trans Am speed away. Bandit looked at Maurice as he ran across the street to where his car was.

"Where you goin'?" he asked.

"To get those fools," he pointed at the Trans Am.

Bandit followed him to the car. The two got in, leaving Keith and Troy battling with the other men. Maurice sped away, hoping his buddies would be okay. He placed his gun in Bandit's lap as he reached in his pocket. He took the clip to the weapon out and placed it in Bandit's lap.

"Reload my clip for me," he said.

Maurice watched as the Trans Am turned a corner. He pulled his .380, took the safety off, and started busting off at the back window as he came up on the fleeing car's back bumper. Bandit reached out the window, and started busting off as well.

A few bullets hit a back tire, and the Trans Am smashed into the back of a Ford EXP that was sitting at a red light.

"Pull up on the side of them so I can get a good shot," Bandit ordered.

Maurice tossed the stick into first gear and jammed on the brakes, stopping right next to the car. Bandit had a clear shot at the driver.

After being hit with shot after shot, the driver's forehead hit the steering wheel. The other man in the car got out and started running. Bandit squeezed the trigger, getting the best shot he possibly could at the man's back, with two shots hitting him. Bandit tried to fire again, but ran out of bullets. Maurice grabbed the 10mm.

"Meet me up the block!" Maurice shouted, jumping out the car.

Maurice went after the man on foot and popped off at him. He hit the man twice, as the guy crossed the street. He picked up speed, running as fast as he could, and grabbed the man by the back of his shirt.

"No!" the guy screamed. "Please, don't kill me! I don't wanna die! Please..." But the sound of gunfire drowned out the man's scream, and after two more shots, death was his new home.

Maurice turned around and saw Bandit approaching quickly in his car. He hopped in the passenger's side and slammed the door shut.

"Run me past my house, I need to get another gun," he told Bandit, looking straight ahead.

Bandit looked at Maurice. He wasn't too thrilled at being ordered around, but he figured they did need more power. Quickly Bandit whipped a u-turn, and drove like a wild man headed toward Maurice's block. With the music on blast, Maurice turned and faced Bandit the moment he stopped at the light. Somehow, he felt bad about his decision. Within a split second, Maurice cocked his gun, and splattered Bandit's brain to pieces.

Without hesitation, Maurice hopped out and dragged Bandit's body to the fence across the alley from his backyard. He hated leaving him near his home, but he figured trash belonged in an alley.

Chapter Sixteen

The red pumps Alvina wore matched the silk dress that clung to her petite frame. She smiled, as she stole a glance at her reflection from a store's front window. Her freshly dyed jet black hair made her look like a teenager. She added a little strut in her walk, as she continued toward her husband's new bistro. Alvina hadn't felt this good in years.

The writing on the window read, *THE GRAND BISTRO,* in large gold and black cursive letters. Alvina felt proud, as she opened the door and went inside. Although she was glad Lemar was out of the game, she still worried about his safety. On numerous occasions she expressed to Lemar how much she hated the fact that his business was in a high crime area, but he was very confident that it didn't matter. So far, things were going well.

When Alvina entered, there were two waitresses placing silverware on tables. Her face lit up, as she spotted Lemar sitting at a corner table, writing something down. He appeared to be in deep concentration.

She knew he felt good to be doing something legal to make money for a change. She walked over and stood in front of the table, wondering when he was going to look up.

Lemar tapped the pen on the table twice, and looked up at the sexy woman in red that now occupied his vision. *My wife is so beautiful*, he thought. "Hey Baby. What are you doing here all dressed up in that sexy dress?"

"This old thing," she replied blushing. "I just came by to see how my businessman was doing."

Lemar laughed. "I'm fine," he said, standing up. He walked around the table, and gently kissed her on the lips.

"So, how does it feel to be doing something positive and honest with your life?" she asked, wanting another kiss from him.

"It feels sort of strange," Lemar said. "It's not the same as hustling, which I still miss. But, I really miss the money."

"I know you do, but this move is for the best."

"I know," Lemar responded. "That life is behind me now."

"I'm so proud of you," she said. She slid her hand on his back, and grabbed a handful of his ass.

They looked into each another's eyes and kissed again.

❈ ❈ ❈

Tia walked in hesitantly, after Maurice agreed to see her. The moment she entered, Maurice kept his eyes on her as she walked to the sofa and sat on the edge, near him.

"So, what brings you here?" Maurice asked bluntly.

"I need to talk to you."

"About?"

"About what happened at the club last week."

Maurice smirked. "So talk." His eyes moved to her stomach, seeing that she was indeed very much pregnant.

"Joe's planning to come Uptown and shoot up Kalhoun Avenue. I'm just lettin' you know before it happens."

"We've been waiting for him and his crew to bring the drama, Tia."

"I've asked him not to go through with it," she said.

"We killed two of his buddies," Maurice said. "I'm sure he

wants to get his revenge."

"But why did this have to happen?" she asked, putting a hand on her forehead.

"You mean you don't know? Tia, you of all people don't have the slightest idea?"

She didn't answer his questions. "So, I've heard you've made quite a name for yourself. You're the most talked about niggah in Uptown these days."

He smiled and spread his arms. "What can I say? The police have made me public enemy number one. And niggahs in the street are scared of me for some reason." He put his hands behind his back and looked at her. "How's your baby doing?" He pointed to her stomach. "How many months are you?"

Tia trembled then swallowed. "Seven months." A tear slid down her face.

"How could you destroy my kid, and justify having some other niggah's baby?"

"Maurice, I wasn't ready for another child back then. I was just trying to get my self together. I told you dat we could have kids in the future when I felt I was ready, but you got so mad at me."

"What difference does it make between then and now? You act like it's been ten years. I would've taken care of my kid."

"How could you take care of a kid if you're going in and out of jail?" she asked.

"Regardless, the kid would've been taken care of, Tia! My mother or Lemar would've helped you with the kid."

"I didn't come here to argue with you, Maurice."

"Well, you shouldn't have shown up at all. Now, get out!"

Tia looked at him, then touched her stomach. She rushed towards the door and opened it.

"Maurice, you're wrong!" she exclaimed. "You're just like my punk ass brother. You're heartless, stupid, clueless and fearless. Brian was so heartless that he'd sell crack to his own mother, and so clueless to fact that his next of kin would kill him for it."

There was something about those words, that didn't register at first, but then like a startling revelation, it came to him. "Did you kill Brian?" he questioned her.

"No, but you wanna know who did?" she asked.

"What do you think?"

"It was Bam," she softly revealed. "I got Bam to do it."

Maurice stood up straight. His eyes appeared to be fixed on Tia's throat. He wondered why Tia would get Bam, the neighborhood snitch to off her brother. Whatever the reason, Maurice considered him dead, and maybe even her.

❈　❈　❈

When Officer Reynolds and Detective Sanders walked into the alley behind Milburn Street, the crime scene was filled with everyone from investigators to the media, who were desperately trying to get the story.

The two of them saw a young man laying on his back, with multiple gunshot wounds to his head and body. The left hand of the murder victim was handcuffed to a fence. "Another damn body," Reynolds said, appearing intoxicated. He had pushed his daily alcohol intake to four times a day after Bailey's murder.

Sanders knelt down beside the body. "An execution style slaying," he said. He got up and walked over to Reynolds. "Things are getting more gruesome in this city by the minute."

"Well, Detective, this is Washington, D.C. This city is known as the Murder Capitol." He looked around the alley. "I think the Patterson residence is right around the corner from here."

"Reynolds, what are you saying?"

"I'm saying, I think you should issue a warrant for Maurice Patterson's arrest."

"But where's our proof?" Sanders asked, waving away the smell of Reynolds breath that reeked of Vodka.

"Look, I have a feeling Maurice did this!" Reynolds shouted, as he pointed at the dead body.

"We can't go around accusing people without evidence, Officer. All we can do for now is investigate, and hope to find some witnesses."

"Can't we at least make Maurice a prime suspect? I'm not saying we have to charge him with anything, just make him a suspect," Reynolds pleaded.

"That's fair enough. I'll go to his house and question him. But remember, Maurice Patterson is not the only violent person around here."

"I know, but look at the nature of the crime, Detective. Patterson's a cutthroat, and only a true cutthroat would kill someone execution style."

"We'll go to his house and have a talk with him." Sanders turned and walked toward another officer. "Does the victim have any I.D.?"

"Yeah, his name is Calvin Sparks," the officer said. "Age twenty-two."

"I know Maurice Patterson did this," Reynolds persisted.

"Look, Officer, we don't have enough evidence to charge him with first-degree murder," Sanders told him. "Even if Maurice pulled the trigger and killed this man, we still can't charge him at this very moment."

"Why?" Reynolds questioned. He looked at the Detective like he was the shooter. It seemed as if the dark circles beneath his eyes, darkened more and more each day. Clearly, the stress was getting to him.

151

Young Assassin

"Because we don't have anything on him, that's why!"
Sanders was starting to loose his patience. "You know how many
people drop dead around here? There are three other murders
around here that Maurice is the primary suspect for, but the evidence on any of them isn't solid enough. It's easy to blame someone for murder, but we can't make an arrest unless the evidence
is substantial. That's the reason why most murders in this city go
unsolved." Sanders patted Reynolds on his back. "Don't worry,
we'll get him. He's got to slip up at some point."

❈   ❈   ❈

Maurice sat on the floor, and looked at his artwork. Just as he
was about to fill in the drawing to give it a little more life, he
heard someone knocking at the front door. He then heard his
father talking with another man. Maurice got up and went downstairs to investigate.

"Maurice, someone's here to see you," Leonard yelled, letting
in two police officers.

Maurice smirked as he saw Officer Reynolds and Detective
Sanders standing in his doorway. "Don't you have anybody else
in the neighborhood to harass? What do you want?" he asked.

"Maurice, we'd like to ask you a few questions," Sanders
said.

"About what?"

"About the murder of a young man that was found in the alley
right behind your house."

Leonard folded his arms, appearing intrigued. "A murder?"

"Oh, your son didn't tell you he goes around killing people,
sir?" Reynolds asked.

Sanders continued. "Maurice, do you know a young man by

the name of Calvin Sparks?"

"Yeah, I know him," Maurice responded. "Everybody calls him Bandit."

"Did you know that he was killed early this morning?" Sanders asked.

"Nah," Maurice said unfazed.

"Why don't you seem surprised?" Reynolds asked.

Maurice shrugged. "You expect violent people to die violently."

Sanders, Reynolds, and Maurice's father all looked at each other. Sanders wrote something down on his notepad, and cleared his throat. "Maurice, do you own a gun?"

Maurice took a few seconds to answer. "Several B.B. guns. I'm too young to own a real gun."

Sanders looked at Leonard. "Sir, would you mind if we searched your home?"

"Are you saying my son is a suspect?" Leonard asked.

"Well, he's one person we're looking at. So, may we search your home?" Sanders asked again.

"Come back with a warrant first," Leonard responded.

"We'll do that, sir," Sanders said.

"That should give you enough time to gather your guns and toss them someplace, huh, Maurice?" Reynolds asked.

"Cool it, Reynolds," Sanders ordered. He looked at Leonard. "Have a good day."

Maurice smiled. He looked at his father as he closed the door. "Dad, see how the police have made me public enemy number one?"

"Maurice, did you kill that boy?" Leonard asked, looking his son straight in the eye.

"Yeah, me and Troy smoked him," Maurice answered.

"What!" Leonard shouted. "Why would you do something like that?"

"Because he was responsible for something that went down a few years ago, so I was just paying him back."

"Are you talking about your kidnapping?" Leonard asked. He remembered Lemar telling him about it a while ago.

"Yeah. It was because of Bandit, that I got kidnapped. If it wasn't for Alvina, I would've been killed. He had to pay in a very unsympathetic way," Maurice replied.

Leonard shook his head. He couldn't believe his son had turned this way. "If you live by the gun, you'll perish by it, Son."

"Dad, I'm not afraid to die. I don't fear death at all."

Leonard stared at his son. "When I was coming up, whenever I had a beef with somebody, I used my hands in a straight brawl."

"That was then and this is now. Times have changed. This ain't the Sixties or Seventies."

"Just what are you trying to prove out here?" Leonard asked. "Just remember, Son, you may be bad, but there's someone out there who's even badder."

Chapter Seventeen

Joe and his two buddies walked to the old station wagon he often drove during drive-bys. Armed with deadly weapons, they planned a quick hit on the Kalhoun Avenue Mob, who had been responsible for the deaths of two of their buddies. They didn't care what the outcome was. They were ready for an all out war.

He and his buddies got into the station wagon, and slammed the doors with vengeance. Joe smiled, hoping that all the members from the K.A.M. would be out there. He knew he wouldn't get them all, but he especially wanted Maurice.

Joe looked at his buddy who was driving. "Let's go get those niggahs."

Maurice sat on top of a mailbox, as he looked across the street at Keith and Troy, who were sharing a blunt. With Bandit finally dead, Maurice could crown himself the street champion. He had done what most people who feared Bandit wouldn't have dreamt of doing.

Suddenly, he saw Bonita coming his way wearing a tight white skirt and a bikini top. *I can't believe she's out here tricking,* he thought.

"Maurice, you got any crack?" Bonita asked.

"Not for you,"

"Come on, Maurice." She touched his arm.

"Bonita, I'm not selling you any rocks!" Maurice yelled.

"Why?"

"Because I said so," he said. "You're Brian's mom." He had

always respected her, and couldn't believe she was a crackhead.

"But why?" she pressed.

Maurice frowned at her. "Because I..."

"Yo, niggahs!" a voice yelled, cutting his sentence short.

Maurice turned and saw an old, gold Plymouth station wagon with tinted windows rolled halfway down, riding up the Avenue in his direction. The first thing he saw were two black guns being held out the window. Maurice grabbed his weapon, removed the safety catch, aimed and fired at the station wagon.

He hopped off the mailbox, getting skinned by a bullet in the process, and took cover behind it. Troy reached for the .32 caliber revolver he had on his waist, and fired.

Maurice stood up, squeezing the trigger, trying to hit the station wagon as it disappeared up the Avenue.

"Is that the fool from The Mojito Ballroom?" Troy asked.

Maurice nodded. "Yeah," he said, holding his left arm where the bullet had skinned him. "We gotta go pay that fool a visit." Maurice looked down by the mailbox and saw Bonita sitting on the ground holding her leg.

"You okay, Bonita?" he asked.

"It doesn't hurt too bad," she said, clenching her teeth.

Maurice reached in his pocket and gave Troy his keys. "Take her to the hospital. My car is parked around the block on Sheridan." His gaze returned to Bonita. "Troy's gonna take you to the hospital. I gotta go."

He looked at Keith, as Troy jogged down the street. So, what we gonna do, Maurice?" Keith asked.

"What do you think?" Maurice glared. "We're gonna go handle some business!" He put his gun on his waist. "Meet me at my house after y'all drop Bonita off."

An hour later, Troy and Keith were sitting on Maurice's bed, as they watched him stuff bullets into the clip of the Mac-Ten he held proudly in his hands. Troy got up and opened the closet door, and couldn't believe how much firearm he saw.

"Go ahead and grab yourself a gun," Maurice boasted. He slapped the clip into the Mac-Ten, cocked it, then showed a crooked smile. "Time to go to work, fellas."

Keith grabbed a 9mm out the closet, to go with the .357 revolver he already had on him. He checked the clip to make sure it was fully loaded.

"I'm ready to let these fools have it," Troy said. He pulled the car keys from out the pocket of his khakis. "Let's go."

"What's the name of the street they live on?" Keith asked.

"Tuscan Street," Troy responded.

Maurice walked out of the room and went downstairs, with his crew following him. Just as he was about to open the front door, Loretta and Leonard walked into the house. They looked at him, then at the deadly weapon in his possession. Troy managed to quickly put his behind his back.

"Where are you going with that thing?" Loretta sternly asked.

Maurice looked into his mother's beautiful green eyes. "I gotta go get somebody," he told her.

"Oh really, well just make sure you don't come back. I guess you've forgotten about what I told you," Loretta said clearly. "I'm sick of this."

Maurice looked at his father as he walked past and went outside. Keith and Troy trailed behind him, closing the door. They walked to Troy's car that was parked out front. They had switched cars, so Joe and his crew couldn't recognize them right away.

As Troy cruised down the street with the convertible top down, he felt the light touch of drizzle coming from the sky. Everyone was silent, as they anticipated what was about to go down. Maurice patted the semi-auto in his lap. The dudes had come up in his hood and tried to take him out, but they'd missed, and now it was payback time.

Young Assassin

Instantly, Troy whipped a sharp turn and headed down a side street. "Here we go," he said, breaking the silence. He looked back at Maurice, who had an expression made of stone.

Troy's Grandville rolled down the street slowly with the lights out. Maurice lifted the semi-auto from his lap. He looked down the street, and saw a group of guys leaning on a fence outside a small housing project. Since it was dark out, he couldn't tell if there were any innocent people out there with them. *Oh well, if somebody's in the wrong place at the wrong time, that's too bad*, he thought.

A few seconds later, Keith pointed both of his guns and fired. People began screaming and ran for cover to avoid being hit. Troy made a sharp left turn, and headed back to their neighborhood in a different direction.

Joe was lying flat on his back, in a bit of a daze as he clenched his heart, while he struggled to get up. The hollow point bullets had struck him like a viper's venom. He looked to his left, and saw one of his friends lying on the ground with opened eyes, as if he were dead. Before Joe died, the thought entered his mind that he should've never tried to confront the K.A.M.

❄ ❄ ❄

Officer Reynolds forced Keith, Troy and a few other neighborhood bullies, to spread their legs and put their hands on their heads. Officers Brown, Casey and Olson were on the scene with him. Two squad cars were parked in the middle of Sixth and Kalhoun Avenue, blocking off the only entrance.

Officer Brown dropped to a knee, lifted Troy's pants leg and reached into his socks. As he pulled out a blunt and a dime bag of weed, he handed it to Officer Reynolds and smiled. Reynolds nodded and looked back at him, shaking his head.

"I'm not going to arrest him for a measly ten dollar bag of pot," he said to Officer Brown. "Did anyone find any crack or weapons on any of them?"

"Nothing," Officer Casey said.

"No weapons or drugs," Officer Olsen confirmed.

"If none of you shot that crackhead, hooker and dope-dealer lying dead on the corner of Second and Kalhoun Avenue, then who the hell did?" Reynolds asked.

"Somebody from Eureka Street did it," a stocky guy spoke up. "Their whole crew is at war wit' us."

Reynolds smirked. "Why?"

"Some guy from around our neighborhood robbed somebody from their neighborhood," the same guy answered.

"We just came from Eureka Street an hour ago, after an apparent senseless shooting," Olson said. "A witness who lives on Eureka Street said someone from the K.A.M. robbed a drug-dealer, then showed back up a short time later, and shot up the neighborhood."

"Well, we don't know anything about that," Troy lied.

"I would bring you all in, but the person who gave us that information won't come to the precinct, for fear of being shot himself," Reynolds said. He walked away, but stopped before he reached the car. "I know it's not possible, but don't kill anybody else before my damn shift is over," he said. The other officers got into their squad cars and drove away.

"We gotta get Bam," Keith said.

"No," Troy replied. "We don't need to add fuel to the fire. Wait until things cool down and then go after Bam. If we start a gun war now, all of us are gonna go down."

"I say we get us a twelve gauge, a Mac-Eleven, and a few 9mms, and go light up Eureka Street with fireworks," Keith said.

"Keith, listen to me," Troy said sternly. "The police already know that we're at odds with the Eureka Street crew. If we do so much as shoot one of them in the leg, they gonna come at all of us with big fat warrants. For once, let's chill out."

"I feel like getting Maurice, so me and him can go handle those fools," Keith said.

"No. It's better not to tell Maurice. You know what he'll do. The police are already breathing down his neck as it is. It would be wiser to get Bam some other time."

"A'ight," Keith responded, not meaning it.

Chapter Eighteen

Maurice aimed his 9mm at the dark sky, and popped off fourteen rounds. Shells dropped into the snow by his dark brown Timberland boots, as steam came from the gun's barrel. Emmit, a youngster from the neighborhood, grinned as he watched his idol. For years, he'd tried to hang out with Maurice, but to no avail, Maurice only allowed him to hang around occasionally.

"Happy New Year," Maurice said to the fellas.

Troy reached into the pocket of the white hoody he had on underneath his Gortex jacket and pulled out his .380. After taking the safety off, he aimed it at the sky and fired seven shots. He happened to catch the expression of J.B.'s face, and raised an eyebrow. "J.B., what's wrong with you?" he asked.

J.B. put his hands in the pockets of his new Philadelphia Eagles jacket and looked at Troy. "Niggahs don't wanna change for the better," he answered.

Maurice looked at J.B. "So, what you saying?" he asked.

J.B. knelt to the ground, and made a snowball. "Nothing," he answered.

"We're just havin' fun," Troy said, putting his gun back.

"That's just it," J.B. said. "Everything to y'all is a bunch of fun!"

"So, since we're busy having fun, and you're so serious these days, is that the reason why we hardly ever see you?" Troy questioned.

J.B. hesitated.

"Answer him," Maurice ordered. He reached down and picked up a shell that had fallen in the snow between his boots.

"Look, I'm trying to get my life together," J.B. explained. "I can't risk hanging wit' y'all in the street. There are niggahs who want y'all dead, and I'm not getting caught in no damn cross fire."

Troy frowned. "What's the difference between now and a few years ago?" he asked.

"Y'all are worse now," J.B. responded. "Maurice has a rep for being a heartless killer, and you're known for being a psychopathic robber."

Keith and Emmit laughed.

"So, you're dissin' your crew?" Troy asked.

J.B. looked at Troy. "No, I'm not," he said. "Maybe if you guys would quit trying to be gangsters, and start doing something positive wit' your lives, then maybe I would start hanging wit' y'all again."

"So, what are you doing that's so great, J.B.?" Maurice asked.

"I'ma submit my application to the Air Force Academy."

"The Air Force?" Troy asked.

"Yup," J.B. said nodding. "Look, I can't find a job, but I'm not gonna use that as an excuse to start hustling again."

The smile left Maurice's face. "Sounds fair enough," he said. "Do what you gotta do."

J.B. stood and threw the snowball he made into someone's backyard. "Let's go inside, it's cold out here."

❄ ❄ ❄

Bonita walked through the smelly, unclean stairwell of her building, on her way to her apartment, where she rested her head in exchange for sexual activity with her landlord, about fifteen to twenty times a month.

As she exited the stairwell, she saw a familiar young man standing at her door.

"Bam, what's up, baby? Got some rock for me?"

"Yeah, but I want some head first," Bam responded.

"Okay," she replied. "The door's open."

He walked in, he saw hundred's of roaches crawling all over the walls. "That's okay. I changed my mind," Bam said frowning.

"What's okay?"

"Getting some head. You got fuckin' roaches crawling all over the place. That's nasty as hell."

"Well, you wanna do it at your place?"

"Nah, my mom's home," he replied. "But you can do me right here in the hallway." He reached into his pocket and showed her a twenty-dollar bag of rock. She scratched her unkempt short blond hair, as she stared at the plastic bag.

"Okay, come on," she agreed.

Bam left the building after he'd finished with Bonita, and walked out into the frigid cold weather, waiting for crackheads to come by and get served. He looked at the dirty snow lying on the ground outside the apartment complex. He walked slowly from in front of the complex, and looked up and down the street. There were no crackheads in sight.

Bam rubbed his hands together, and thought about going to get his winter coat, but quickly noticed a familiar face heading up the sidewalk.

Emmit, wearing a bright red coat spotted Bam. He stopped and looked at him briefly, before passing by. At first he contemplated on running for his life, but quickly realized it was his only chance to earn Maurice's respect. Emmit had agreed to kill Bam in order to earn his place in the K.A.M. crew. He reached in his coat for his .32, sneaked a peek back at him, and saw Bam looking at him with resentment in his eyes.

As Emmit walked to the front of the building, Bam spoke. "Where do you think you goin', fool?"

Emmit shivered, but tried to play hard. "You don't wanna fuck with me,"

"You comin' on my turf to sell drugs? 'Cause if you are, I'ma kill you. Get out my fuckin' neighborhood while you have the chance."

Emmit looked at the bob hairdo wearing fool with such contempt, that it looked as if he was about to spill his blood right there. "The K.A.M. will come up here, take out your whole crew, and then take over things."

"I don't think so," a voice said from behind him.

Before Emmit could turn around to see who it was, there was a gun to his head, and the person had taken his gun from his waist.

"Should I kill him, Bam?" the guy asked.

Bam smiled and walked to where the member of his crew had Emmit under control. "You ain't talkin' so tough now," he said to Emmit. He looked at his buddy. "Let him go and give me his gun, Darnell."

Darnell, a dark-skinned short guy, with a white knitted hat on, pushed Emmit down on the icy walkway, and gave the revolver to Bam.

Emmit lay on the ground for a few seconds, before getting off the ground. "Give me my gun, you faggot!" he said harshly.

"What did you call me, motherfucka?" Bam questioned. He aimed the gun at Emmit's chest then lowered it, as he looked at Darnell. "Shoot this niggah, Darnell!" He sniffed the cold air and laughed.

Emmit looked at Darnell and smirked, as if daring him to do so. Darnell aimed his weapon and shot him in his left thigh. Emmit yelled uncontrollably. He couldn't believe he'd been shot.

"Shoot him again, Darnell!" Bam commanded, looking down at Emmit with a smile on his face.

"Nah, that's enough to warn those niggahs," Darnell said.

"Let's go," Bam said, eyeing Darnell. He glanced down at Emmit. "Tell the K.A.M. if they want a war, they know where to find me." He and Darnell walked away, leaving their adversary wounded and hurt.

Emmit tried to stand, but slipped and fell chin first to the ground. He struggled up the sidewalk, crawling on the snowy ice with the wind at his back. He heard his pager go off. He thought about Maurice, Troy and Keith, who would no doubt bring the heat, as Maurice called it, after he informed them of what happened. He wondered if those two guys were trying to die, by letting him live. *Stupid*, he thought. *They should've killed me.*

❄ ❄ ❄

Maurice was sweating like crazy, as he did the fifth set of push-ups on his bare knuckles in the living room. Lemar and Alvina sat on the sofa, splitting their attention from the television to Maurice.

At that moment, they heard several knocks at the door. "I'll get it," Lemar said. When he opened it, he saw Keith zipping down his suede coat.

"What's up, Keith?"

"What's up, Lemar?" Keith spoke. "Maurice here?"

"Yeah. Come in."

Maurice stepped up to the doorway. "What's going on?"

"Trouble," Keith responded.

"Come up to my room." He led the way upstairs to his bedroom.

165

"Some fool from Eureka Street shot Emmit," he told Maurice, once they were in his bedroom.

"You know who it was?" Maurice asked, with raised eyebrows.

"Emmit said it was some dude named Darnell, that was told by Bam to shoot him. You ready to handle it?" Keith said.

"You ain't said nothing but a word," Maurice said. "Let me get my .38 and coat."

"So what we gonna do?"

"Run up into Bam's apartment and get him."

"You know what apartment he lives in?"

"No, but I know somebody who does."

❋ ❋ ❋

Bonita walked back into her trashy apartment in a daze. She'd been wearing the same old dirty T-shirt for the past week. She tried to remember to keep herself, and her place clean, but she didn't have the mentality to do so. She heard the phone ringing, and went into the dining room to answer it.

"Hello."

"Bonita, what's up?"

"Who this?" she asked.

"Maurice. I need you to do me a big favor."

"What?" she asked excitedly. *Maybe he'll give me what I need*, she thought.

"Tell me what apartment Bam lives in."

"What's in it for me?"

"Rock," he said to her.

"Meet me in front of my building in fifteen minutes."

"Cool." Maurice hung up the phone, and looked at Keith. "It's time to put in some work."

Maurice parked his car around the back of Oak Terrace, in an empty alley beside three huge dumpsters. He and Keith got out the car and walked around to the front. As they turned the corner, they saw Bonita standing in front of her building shivering. It felt odd to Maurice to approach this place without going to see Brian or Tia.

"Hey, Bonita," he said, as they walked up to her. "You got that information?"

"You got the rock?"

Maurice looked at Keith. "Go ahead and give it to her."

Keith reached into the pocket of his coat and gave her a nickel bag of crack. "There you go," he said.

"Now what apartment building does Bam live in, Bonita?" Maurice asked, with authority.

"Building Three, Apartment Six," she said, anxious to get back into her apartment to smoke.

"Thanks. Come on, Keith," Maurice replied.

They left Bonita and went to Building Three and stood outside the glass door. Keith pulled the door open. "Let's go on up."

Maurice looked behind him, to see if there was anybody around. "Okay, go ahead. I'm right behind you." He grabbed his revolver from between his hip and belt.

Keith ran up the stairs, pulling out his .357 Magnum in the process. As he approached the apartment, he knocked on the door and squatted down, as Maurice moved out of view of the peephole.

"Who is it?" a boyish voice asked.

"I need some coke," Maurice said, trying to sound like some pressed crackhead.

Like a magic code, the door instantly opened. Keith busted a single shot to the ceiling, as Maurice stepped into view and saw Bam looking wild as ever. As he turned to run, he caught a bullet in his arm. Maurice and Keith pursued him, firing shots that hit the walls and a china cabinet, as Bam ran in an opened bedroom and slammed the door behind him.

The sound of a woman's scream came from the room, as Keith and Maurice fired shots at the door, putting hole after hole in it, until they ran out of bullets.

Maurice cursed under his breath. "Come on, let's roll," he said to Keith, wishing they'd brought more firearm with them. The two dashed out the apartment, down the staircase, and into the alley.

Bam collapsed on the floor after the gunfire ceased. His mother came over to him and touched his arm, seeing blood spilling from out of three wounds in his back. She grabbed the phone, and dialed 911.

"911, how can I help you?" the operator said.

"Yes," she shouted, gripping the threads of the white night-gown she had on. "My son's been shot, and he's lying on my bedroom floor bleeding to death! I live in the Oak Terrace projects, Building Three, Apartment Six! Please hurry!"

"An ambulance crew are on their way," the operator responded.

She hung up the phone and looked at Bam, as his eyes blinked.

Chapter Nineteen

Darnell stood outside Oak Terrace, waiting for his clientele to come pass to do a little early morning shopping. Bam had regained consciousness after three days, but was still listed in critical condition at Washington Hospital Center. Darnell wished now he hadn't shot Emmit days ago. *The whole idea was stupid,* he thought.

Just then a man came over to him and said, "You have any rock?"

Darnell looked at him. He was a fat and out-of-shape looking black man, shivering with a squalid Converse sweatsuit on that looked like it hadn't been washed in years.

"Yeah, I'll hook you up." Just as he reached for the supply in his coat pocket, he felt a metal object on his wrist.

"You're under arrest for dealing drugs, you stupid fool," the man who happened to be an undercover said, cuffing him. "You're coming with me."

Darnell was taken down to the Fourth District Precinct and booked, before being pushed into a small cell with a single bed in it. The undercover came walking by with a short, white woman dressed in a police uniform.

"You caught a dealer?" the female officer asked.

"Yeah, Casey," the undercover said. "He tried to sell me some crack right outside Oak Terrace."

"Oak Terrace?" she asked. "Isn't that where that boy was shot three times in the back, after some guys ran up in his mother's apartment?"

"Yeah. Any leads?"

"Maurice Patterson did it," Darnell blurted out, from inside his cell.

Officer Casey turned around to look at him. "Patterson? What's your proof?"

He spilled the beans about what happened in front of Oak Terrace when Bam told him to shoot some guy.

"Did you see Maurice Patterson Emmit?"

"No, but I know he did it. Bam told me some light-skinned dude named Keith, we know from the K.A.M., who robbed him last year, also shot him when they ran up in the apartment. They were tryna kill him," Darnell replied.

"Are you sure it was Patterson?" Casey asked.

"He had a motive," the undercover interrupted.

"He's the K.A.M.'s main triggerman, and the guy I shot is a member of his posse," Darnell said.

"That should be enough to charge him," Casey said, with a grin. "Well, the only thing to do now is to inform the Sergeant about this. Send someone to arrest Maurice Patterson now!"

❄   ❄   ❄

Loretta and Maurice sat at the dining room table, discussing whether or not Maurice would be allowed back in the house for good. Leonard abruptly walked by, giving his wife an evil eye.

"What would you like for dinner, Leonard?" Loretta asked, not wanting to discuss the matter any further.

"Just vegetables," he answered, noticing Maurice watching his every move.

"I'll start dinner right away," she said. On her way toward the kitchen, there was a knock at the door. "I'll get it," Loretta said.

by Mike G

"Who's there?" she asked.

"District of Columbia Police Department."

Loretta looked back at Maurice, closed her eyes, and said a quiet prayer as she opened the door. She looked into the familiar face of Detective Sanders, and a few police whom she'd seen before.

"Can I help you?"

"Yes, Mrs. Patterson, is Maurice home?" Detective Sanders asked. He pulled on the collar of his coat.

What has Maurice done now? Loretta stared at him for a second, contemplating on telling a lie that Maurice wasn't home, and that she didn't know where he was. But very reluctantly she said, "Yes."

Detective Sanders and two officers walked inside the house and into the living room. "Maurice," he said.

Maurice looked at the detective without concern. "What do you want?"

"You're under arrest for the attempted murder of Bam Pruitt."

Leonard stared at the scene in disbelief, as the woman officer forced his son up and handcuffed him. He caught a glimpse of Loretta shaking her head in complete sadness.

"You have the right to remain silent," Sanders said. "If you give up that right, anything you say can and will be used against you in a court of law. You have the right to an attorney. If you can not afford an attorney, one will be appointed to you." He looked at Casey. "Take him to the squad car."

Darnell sat in the office of Detective Sanders, who looked at him with an evil stare, wondering why he'd been brought there.

Young Assassin

The sounds of fingers tapping the keys of a typewriter in the other room could be heard. He looked at the clock.

"Do you have to go somewhere, Darnell?" Detective Sanders asked.

"No, I just wanted to see what time it was."

"Do you know why you were brought here?"

"No."

"You're gonna do the Police Department a little favor. Maurice Patterson is in custody, and being escorted to Central Cell as we speak."

Darnell sat up straight in his chair as he looked at the detective. "What kind of favor?"

"I'll make you a deal. If you become a witness against Maurice, I'll drop the distribution of cocaine charge against you."

"You know he'll deny doing anything, man," Darnell said. "Remember, you're charging him on a hunch that I have. I didn't witness anything."

"But you know the motive behind the shooting," Sanders told him. "That's what counts the most."

Darnell thought for a moment. "Okay, I'll do it."

Chapter Twenty

As he drove Uptown in the cold March afternoon, Lemar thought about going to his stash to get some hush money for the people who would testify against his little brother. He couldn't stand seeing Maurice locked up, and Lemar knew he had the power to get him released.

Ryan Dalby had showed Lemar the written statement given to Maurice by a court referee. One of the people who were going to testify was some guy named Darnell Braxton, and the other was Bam Pruitt. Lemar had heard that Bam was confined to a wheelchair, and would never walk again. He had to find a way to pay Bam and Darnell off. *Everybody has their price*, he thought.

Lemar began to think about his own life, as he looked up at the sky through the windshield. A lot was going on in his life. After marrying Alvina, he'd decided to return to college and pursue a B.S. degree, at Maryland University. His business was doing so well, he had to get Alvina to help run the bistro, while he attended classes.

When he rode up on Eureka Street, he saw an ambulance and several police cars scattered all over the block. Lemar turned off his car and got out. He fastened his brown leather coat and walked to where a short officer stood in the street.

"Excuse me, Officer," Lemar said, the heels of his size twelve dress shoes clicking against the pavement.

The officer turned around. "Yes?"

"What's going on?"

"Same story, just a different day," he replied. "Someone got shot" the officer said, and turned back around.

Just then, Lemar saw Officer Reynolds standing in front of the apartment complex. Smirking to himself, he went over to him.

"Hello, Officer Reynolds," Lemar said.

Reynolds turned around, and his eyes nearly popped out of his head. "What are you doing here, bum?"

"What happened?"

"Again, what are you doing here, Patterson?" Reynolds questioned him.

"Someone who lives in the complex works as a waitress at my bistro, and she hasn't been to work in a while. I came by to see if she's okay," Lemar responded.

"You own a bistro?" Reynolds asked. "What's that Patterson, some kind of cover-up for your illegal activities?"

Lemar reached into his coat pocket and took out his wallet. He pulled a business card and handed it to Reynolds. "I'm legit." He sighed. "So, what happened here?"

Reynolds snatched the card, looked at it, and put it in his pants pocket. "Darnell Braxton, the man who was supposed to testify against your brother, was stabbed in the stomach twice and shot three times in the head," Reynolds replied. He pointed to the bloody white sheet covering the dead body. "So, that's another one of your brother's witnesses dead."

Lemar shook his head and walked away. He knew Maurice couldn't have done it because he was behind bars.

"Hey, Patterson?" Reynolds said.

"What?"

"We're still investigating the murder of Officer Bailey. I was wondering if you could help us out. Would you happen to know anything about that?"

"I don't know anything. I can't help you there," Lemar responded.

"I didn't think so," Reynolds said. "What about Calvin Sparks aka Bandit? You know anything about his death?"

"Nope." He turned to go.

"I thought you were here to check on one of your employees?"

"You know, I think it would be more appropriate to call first." He smiled at Reynolds then walked back to his car.

❀ ❀ ❀

Officer Reynolds went inside the judiciary building on his lunch hour. After going up to the fourth floor, he went down a short hallway with framed pictures of artwork on the walls. He stopped at a brown wooden door with bronze letters on it that read, *Public Official Joshua Weinberg*. He knocked three times.

"Come in," he heard the prosecutor say.

Reynolds went in and closed the door behind him. His attention was immediately directed toward a painting of the Prophet Moses cutting a path through the Red Sea, as he entered.

Weinberg stood up and unloosened his necktie. "Officer, I'm sure you have a good reason for being here," he said.

Reynolds looked at him. "Sir, one of the witnesses in the Pruitt case was murdered a while ago."

Weinberg's pale face reddened. "Damn! Son of a bitch!" He went over to the window, then turned to look at Reynolds. "Is Pruitt okay?"

"I think so. But I think it would be wise to place him in a witness protection program."

"Do you really think Pruitt is going to show up for court to testify?"

"I'm really not sure," Reynolds replied. "Pruitt is handi

capped now, and he's a witness — which is a better reason to place him in the protection program. Because he's in a wheelchair, it makes him an easier target for a bullet."

"I don't think he'll testify against Maurice Patterson or Keith Lewis," Weinberg said.

"Who do you want more, Patterson or Lewis?"

"Mr. Maurice Patterson, of course. Keith Lewis just shows up every now and then. He's not a real threat."

"In that case, I have an idea," Reynolds said.

"What's your idea?"

"We've been investigating the execution style slaying of Calvin Sparks aka Bandit, which I think Patterson committed, as well as my former partner, William Bailey's fatal shooting. I know in my heart that Maurice Patterson is responsible for both of them. Can't we charge him with murder in these cases?"

Weinberg sighed helplessly. "We can file charges all we want on both those killings, but the fact remains there's still no witnesses to testify against Patterson. If we made those homicides into murder cases, he'd win both. The chances of us winning any of those cases are slim to none. And in the Pruitt case, I don't even think slim came to town."

"Can't we try, just to keep him off the streets?"

"I'm afraid not," Weinberg said.

"Why?" Reynolds whined. He threw his hands in the air.

"Because we'd be trying to avoid the inevitable."

Reynolds sighed. "You're not sounding like a prosecutor."

"You can't deny that I'm making sense," Weinberg said.

"Sir, with all due respect, I do believe I came up with a good idea."

"I know you did." Weinberg walked behind his desk and took a seat. "But in the meantime, go to Pruitt's home and have a talk with him. Persuade him to enter into the program like you said. If he doesn't want to testify, then the U.S. Attorney's Office has no

choice but to drop the attempted murder charges against Lewis
and Patterson."

❀   ❀   ❀

Bam rested uneasily in his electrical wheelchair, as he looked
at the news. More and more murders were being reported
throughout the city everyday. A small wisp of fear flowed
through him, as he thought about what had transpired in front of
Darnell's building just hours ago. Maurice and his crew were
quite wicked — probably the most ruthless guys in Uptown. He
didn't know whether to testify against them or not.

At that moment, he heard someone knock on the door. He
steered to the dining room table and grabbed his Grimaldi .380
caliber handgun, and put his finger on the trigger.

"Who is it?" he asked.

"Officer Charles Reynolds, D.C.P.D."

Bam steered the wheelchair to the door and reached for the
top and bottom locks. He unlocked them, then put the wheelchair
in reverse.

"It's open," he said, pointing his gun directly at the front door.

When Officer Reynolds entered the apartment, he flinched.

"What the fuck! Put the gun down, son!" he ordered, as he
reached for his own piece.

Bam lowered his firearm and swallowed.

"You shouldn't have done that," Reynolds said.

"Well, ever since Maurice and Keith shot me, I don't trust
anybody."

"Well you need to come up with another fucking plan,"
Reynolds replied, as he closed the door and put the locks back
on.

"Why are you here anyway?" Bam asked.

"I'm here to offer you protection." Reynolds pulled out a flask, and took a swallow of his Vodka and orange juice. At this point, he didn't care who saw him drinking. He was beyond stressed. "After all, you're a witness, and if you intend to testify against Maurice, you need to be placed into a witness protection program."

Bam shook his head, steered the wheelchair toward the table, and put the gun on top of it. "I don't wanna testify."

"Why not?" Reynolds asked.

"I have my mother to think about," Bam said. "You gonna protect her too? Maurice Patterson is a fucking maniac. It's rumored that he and his crew fired shots at this dude, Bandit's, casket outside the funeral home. Those niggahs are crazy."

Reynolds looked at him. "Is Bandit's real name, Calvin Sparks?"

"I think so. Why?"

"No reason," Reynolds answered. "You do plan to testify against him, don't you?"

"I'm sorry officer, I can't," Bam said. "Those fools from the K.A.M. might shoot my mother or something. You can't protect her."

"Yes, we can," Reynolds said, getting upset.

Bam lowered his head. "I love my mother, and I'd rather go to jail for perjury or contempt of court, than to see her killed."

Reynolds placed one of his hands on his chin. "Have it your way then." He took a few steps toward the living room, and turned around. "Will you at least testify against Lewis?"

"You mean Keith?" Bam swallowed, as he thought it over. "No. If I testify against one, I might as well testify against them both."

"Well, then," Officer Reynolds said, walking toward the door, "Patterson and Lewis will go free, and will continue to plague this community. It's to the point now the police will have to take the law into our own hands." He took the locks from off the door and opened it, while looking back at Bam. "Come and lock the door," he said.

Bam steered toward the door and shut it, as he heard the officer's footsteps echo in the stairwell.

❊   ❊   ❊

Ryan Dalby and two police officers walked inside the D.C. jail, and were escorted to an elevator by a correctional officer. When they reached the seventh floor, they got off and walked down a bright corridor, past a library, en route to a small cellblock around the corner. As soon as the double doors were unlocked, Ryan instantly interpreted loud screams from down the next corridor, as a prison rape was in progress.

Finally they reached the room where Maurice and Keith were being held. "You're out of here," Ryan said to Maurice and Keith. He walked toward the prison bars that separated them. "The charges were dropped."

Maurice stood up from off a dingy cot he was sitting on, with a huge smile. "What do those cops want?" he asked his lawyer, as the correctional officer opened the cell.

"Yeah, why are the charges being dropped?" Keith asked, as he gazed in Ryan's direction with confusion.

"Darnell Braxton was killed," Ryan responded, as he looked at the police officers.

"When?" Maurice asked.

"That's not important. All you need to be concerned with is that the police can't hold you because the prosecution's case is wrecked without Braxton's testimony."

"Why are the police here?" Maurice questioned again.

"They just want you to answer a question," Ryan replied.

When Maurice stepped into the hallway, one of the police officers that he'd recognized from the Fourth District Precinct got into his personal space.

"What?" Maurice asked, looking at the officer.

"Who killed Darnell Braxton?" the officer asked.

"Look, I'm locked up in here, aren't I? How am I supposed to know who he had beef with?"

"It's funny, because he was supposed to testify against you and Keith, and never got the chance to," the officer said.

"Look, I didn't have anything to do with those Oak Terrace dudes," Maurice said, looking for Ryan to interrupt. "Just like I didn't have nothing to do with Bam Pruitt. There's no telling who those dudes pissed off. The Oak Terrace Crew commits heinous crimes, but you don't harass them. But when they get all shot up, you point the finger at me."

"No more questions," Ryan said to the officers.

"Because he did it!" the policeman yelled. He turned to Keith. "What about you?" he asked. "You know anything?"

"Look, the attempted murder charges have been dropped, officer," Ryan said to him." He turned to Keith. "Keith, you don't have to say anything either. You and Maurice have been exonerated."

❃   ❃   ❃

Officer Reynolds stood quietly outside on D Street, and watched Maurice and Keith follow their lawyer to a van parked inside the visitor's parking lot near the gate. The situation with Maurice Patterson was growing dire. People were refusing to come forward it seemed with every crime that he was charged with.

by Mike G

As much as he wanted to protect this city and its citizens, Officer Reynolds knew there was only one way to handle Maurice, and that was to kill him. Because of that, he was growing more and more obsessed with Maurice, just like Officer Bailey had grown obsessed with Lemar at one time. Although he couldn't prove it, Reynolds knew that the obsession that Bailey had with Lemar, had ultimately killed his former partner.

As he thought about it, it scared him. *I guess that's what it means to protect and serve*, he thought. *The worse thing that can happen is they put me on administrative leave without pay. Shit, I can deal with that if it means that motherfucka will be off the street.*

A psychotic smile played around his lips as he watched the van leave the premises.

"You're mine, Maurice," Officer Reynolds said out loud. "Your ass is mine."

Young Assassin

Chapter Twenty—One

Loretta looked at Maurice, who sat at the dining room table drawing a picture. She was impressed by how much of a good artist her son had become. *Wasted talent*, she thought. Loretta waited for him to look in her direction. After several minutes, he never looked up. She got up and walked into the dinning room, and grabbed the drawing.

"What's up, Ma?" Maurice asked calmly. He wondered what was bothering her.

"Why does something have to be up?" Loretta asked.

"Ma, I know you well enough to know you want something. I could see you looking at me from the other room. What's on your mind?"

Loretta smiled. "I guess you know me well, huh?" She put the drawing down, and looked at her son. "Do you remember when you were kidnapped?"

Maurice nodded, experiencing temporary anger, as he remembered that he'd been drawing a picture just before being abducted over three years ago. "Of course, I remember," he said to her. "I'll never forget it."

"I was so scared that you'd been hurt, even killed," Loretta said.

"Ma, what's your point?" he asked, standing up. Talking about the incident always made him irritable.

"The point I'm trying to make is that you have a better chance of dying now, than you did then."

"Ma, are you throwing me out again?"

The idea had crossed her mind a lot lately. "No," she told him. "We've already had that conversation when I let you come back."

"Then what do you want from me?" Maurice asked.

"I want you to stop what you're doing."

"Ma, I'm in way too deep," Maurice said, with a nod. "It's too late for me."

"No it isn't! That's bullshit, and you know it!"

"Ma, you didn't have to deal with the peer pressure when you were growing up like I do. You didn't have to deal with friends getting killed. You never knew what it felt like to have an absentee father, who walked out your life when you were eleven, and popped back up out of nowhere. You don't know what's it like to feel hate after being kidnapped."

Loretta nodded and bit her bottom lip. She could feel her son's pain. "You're right, son," she replied. "I don't know what it felt like to experience any of that when I was young. But you don't have to let it control you. You don't need to allow that negativity to make you give up on life either. All you need to change is your negative attitude. You have to let go of all your anger."

"So, now I have a negative attitude?"

Loretta was silent for a moment before she answered. "Hell yes, you do. You have to learn how to control your attitude in order to control your circumstances, Maurice. Not the other way around."

"Ma, it's too late for me," he said again.

"No, it isn't. This community needs to be cleansed of drugs and violence."

"You sound like it's my fault our society is all messed up."

"That's not what I'm saying, Maurice. You can either repent or perish."

"Our society was all messed up before I came on the scene," Maurice went on.

184

"Of course it was. But you can change and pull yourself together."

"Ma, I gotta go." Maurice was tired of hearing his mother preach.

Loretta and Maurice locked gazes for moment, before he walked toward the front door and left.

❊　❊　❊

Alvina walked to the end of the bar, where Lemar sat reading a magazine. She couldn't believe it when she saw him with a cigarette between his fingers.

"When did you start smoking?" Alvina questioned.

Lemar took his eyes off the magazine and looked at her. "I take a puff every now and then."

Her stance softened a bit. "Do you want something to drink?" she asked, grabbing a glass from behind the bar. She filled it with ice, and fixed him a Remy and Coke, before sliding it in front of him.

"Thanks." He smiled and looked into her slanted eyes, as she stood with her arms folded across her chest.

"You know our anniversary is approaching, don't you?" she asked.

He nodded. "Yes, I know, and have I ever told you that you've been a wonderful wife?" Lemar asked, grabbing the glass.

"I don't think you have," Alvina replied, with a smile. "I try to be the best wife to my husband I possibly can be."

"And I try to be the best husband to my wife I possibly can be," he replied. Lemar smoked the cigarette down to the filter and placed it in the astray.

"I'm so glad I found someone like you, Lemar. I can't wait to have our son or daughter."

"I can't wait either."

As Alvina was putting the bottle of alcohol back on the shelf, she saw a man wearing a blue jean shirt and pants approaching them. He sat six stools down from Lemar, and kept looking in her husband's direction. She went over to him, as she watched Lemar sip on his drink.

"Sir, may I get you something?"

"I'd like a job application and a root beer, please," the man replied.

"Lemar, can you get this man an application?" Alvina asked.

Lemar put the glass down and looked at the man strangely, as he walked in the direction of his office. Suddenly his face turned into a hideous frown. "Martin, get the hell out of my restaurant!" he shouted.

"Didn't Ms. Patterson teach you any manners, Lemar?" Martin said, with a smile on his face. "I haven't seen you in five years, and this is how you treat me? I thought we were friends."

"If you don't get the hell outta here, I'm gonna throw your ass out," Lemar said, taking steps in Martin's direction.

"Are you threatening me? I haven't done anything to you, Lemar. If you're still mad for what happened in the past, I had to do what I had to do. My jail time would've been ten years. Instead, they gave me three after I snitched on you. After all this time, I knew you wouldn't forget, but I thought you would've at least forgiven me."

"Get out!" Lemar shouted.

"What a way to treat a customer and old friend," Martin replied.

"We're not friends anymore!" Lemar yelled. "Now, I'd appreciate it if you'd leave."

"I'll leave after I've paid for my root beer and received my application."

Lemar looked at Alvina. "Honey, give him a root beer, so he can get the hell out." His gaze returned to Martin. "As for the application, we're not hiring."

"Oh really. Well, I saw an ad in the paper that said you were hiring." Martin paused for a moment. "So, you still dealing, Lemar?"

Is this niggah wearing a wire or something, he thought. "I don't deal drugs anymore, Martin, those days are behind me."

"Look, I came here to ask you for a job and to make amends."

"I don't want or need your friendship," Lemar replied.

Alvina placed the glass of root beer in front of Martin.

Martin put his hand in his pocket, pulled out a couple of dollars and placed them on the counter. "How's your brother, Maurice, doing?"

Before Lemar could respond, Martin continued. "Oh, that's right, that lil niggah is out here killing everybody. Well, did you know I'm a witness in one of his slayings, Lemar? I'd hate to go to the police and have him put away."

Alvina swallowed, as she listened to the harsh conversation.

"You don't wanna mess with Maurice. Besides, you're probably lying like shit," Lemar said.

Martin took a sip of the root beer. "If you do me a favor, I'll do you an even bigger one." He paused for a moment before looking back at Lemar. "Now, do I have a job or what?"

Lemar sighed and looked toward Alvina. "Honey, get him an application for me." He turned to Martin. "What killing are you talking about?"

"What if I told you that I saw Maurice go into that alley off Ninth and Kalhoun ten minutes before Officer Bailey was killed?"

"That's such bullshit!" Lemar shouted, as he stood up and pointed at Martin in emphasis. "Even if you did, you didn't see him pull the trigger."

"Maybe I did, maybe I didn't," he teased. "But that depends on you, doesn't it? And to top it all off, I'll be working for the man who put the hit on the officer."

"Why are you playing with your life like this?" Lemar asked Martin.

"You threatening me, Lemar? You gonna put a contract out on me?"

"I'm not gonna do anything to you. It's Maurice you need to worry about."

Alvina left from behind the bar, hoping that her husband was wise enough not to throw any menacing threats at the man. She walked to Lemar's office, wondering if this guy named Martin was lying, but because of her brother-in-law's notorious rep for being a thug, she believed that what he told Lemar could indeed be true.

"I still think you're bullshitting," Lemar said sternly.

"Maybe I am, and maybe I'm not," Martin teased again.

Chapter Twenty-Two

Troy walked into the bistro, and headed to the bar where Lemar was sitting on a stool, talking to one of his chefs. He walked up and took a seat beside him. After the chef walked away, Troy tapped Lemar on the shoulder and smiled.

Lemar returned the expression. "Hey, Troy. What's happening?"

"Nothing but the rent," Troy said. "I'm looking for a job."

"Are you serious?"

"Yeah, man, I'm tryna change my life because it's getting crazy out in the streets."

Well, you came to the right place, because I have a vacancy for a bartender. How old are you?"

"Twenty-one."

"Well, why don't you go behind the bar and get acquainted with the drinks, and practice being a bartender for the rest of the day. By tomorrow, you'll have the job."

"Damn, just like that? How much does the job pay?"

"It pays nine twenty-three an hour. I'll give you an application to take home before we close, but keep in mind, you'll have to take classes at a bartending school later."

"No problem. Thanks, Lemar," Troy said, giving him a pound.

"Don't mention it, Troy."

Troy walked behind the bar, and admired the bottles on the shelf. "Oh, I went to see Seth today," Troy said, picking up a bottle of Hennessey.

"Oh, yeah? How's he doing?"

"He's okay."

"I miss him being around," Lemar said. "Seth and I had a lot of fun growing up."

"Lemar, I'm gonna take a five minute break," a voice said from behind him.

Both Troy and Lemar turned to look at Martin Reed, who looked like he'd been a chef for years in the uniform he wore. Troy's eyes widened as he looked at the traitor, then back at Lemar.

"Hello, Troy," Martin said.

Troy just looked at Martin, appearing a bit bewildered. "Lemar, what's up?" He pointed to Martin.

"Go ahead and take a break, Martin," Lemar said.

Martin smiled at Troy, as he took a pack of cigarettes out his pocket, and walked away.

"Lemar, what the fuck is he doing working here?" Troy smirked.

"He blackmailed me into giving him a job," Lemar whispered to him.

"What?"

"He said he saw Maurice kill Officer Bailey, and was gonna go to the cops unless I gave him a job. Another thing is he might be working undercover in order to find out if I'm still hustling."

"Well, you know what I think?" Troy asked, looking serious.

"Let me guess, you want to have him killed?"

"Yup. And you know what, he's lying to you. I'm the one who helped Maurice lure Officer Bailey into the alley, and I didn't see anyone around before Maurice popped his fat ass."

"But what if he isn't lying? He knows I hate his ass for what he did to me and your brother a long time ago, and that alone makes me wanna have him eliminated," Lemar replied.

"Well, it sounds like he wants to die," Troy said. "And if I can help it, I won't let him do Maurice like that."

"Martin's not that dumb, Troy. He knows he won't live long if he does some dirt like that."

"Have you told Maurice about this?"

Lemar shook his head. "No, and I don't plan to."

"Why?"

"Because he's already being sought after by the police as it is," Lemar explained.

"Well, I'll...never mind."

"You'll what?"

Troy looked over to where people were being seated by the hostess. "Get him myself."

Lemar paused for a moment. He knew Troy was still angry at Martin for setting up his brother. "You really need to let that situation go, Troy."

"I tried to forget all about it, but I can't." Troy immediately thought of Seth, who told him to leave Martin alone if he ever saw him again. "Maurice is a part of my crew and he's a great friend. I'm not gonna stand by and allow a punk like Martin have the power of deciding Maurice's destiny."

Lemar sighed. "I'm not encouraging you to do something wrong, but all I can say is do what you gotta do."

Troy nodded. "Lemar, you can best believe I will."

Later that night, Lemar locked the door to his bistro and followed Alvina outside. "Go ahead and get the car," he said, handing her the keys to the BMW M3. He looked to his left, and spotted a man approaching him.

"Lemar Patterson?" the man asked, flashing a police badge.

Lemar studied him for a moment, then nodded. "Yeah, I'm Lemar Patterson. Who are you?"

"I'm Detective Sanders, D.C.P.D. I'd like to ask you a few questions concerning the murder of Officer William Bailey."

Lemar sucked his teeth. "Hurry up will you, I haven't got all day."

Young Assassin

"Are you aware that your brother has been suspected of Officer Bailey's murder?"

"No, I'm not."

"Well, he has. We have reason to believe that someone put a contract out on Officer Bailey to have him killed, and we also believe that someone is you."

Lemar smiled at the man. "Look, Detective, I don't know who killed Officer Bailey. And why would I have him killed?"

"Because he allegedly planted evidence on you."

Lemar looked Sanders up and down. "I don't have time for this," he said, and stepped away.

Sanders looked at Lemar sternly. "Have a good night." He turned and walked back in the direction he had come from.

Lemar watched him walk away until he'd got into a black Crown Victoria and drove away. As Alvina pulled up, Lemar got in the passenger side and closed the door.

"Who was that?" Alvina asked.

"Trouble," Lemar said to her.

"What?"

"Just trouble. The police aren't letting their guard down concerning Maurice." He looked at Alvina. "I think they're trying to bring him up on yet another murder charge."

❖ ❖ ❖

Troy walked down Kalhoun Avenue with a smile, happy that Lemar had hired him. Suddenly, he heard a loud whistle and then heard somebody call his name. He turned around, and saw Emmit, getting out of a brand new burgundy Ford Bronco with a slight limp.

"Hey, what's up, partner?"

"Nothing much," Emmit said.

Troy looked at the driver of the truck before he pulled off. He instantly became angry.

"Emmit, do you know who that was?" he asked

"Yeah, this hustler named Martin."

"Hustler?"

"Yeah. He just sold me some rocks wholesale."

Troy couldn't believe Martin was back in the game. "Look, Emmit, don't mess with that dude."

Emmit frowned and wiped his sweaty face on the front of his blue T-shirt. "Why? What's up?"

"Look, Martin ain't nothing but trouble."

"What are you talking 'bout?"

Troy told Emmit everything about Martin concerning Lemar, Seth, and what he'd learned today. "I'm telling you to leave that fool alone."

"Damn, I've been messing wit' him for weeks. I see him out here on Kalhoun Avenue all the time. So, he's not cool?"

"No. As a matter of fact, me and Maurice are gonna do away with him."

"When?"

"It could happen tonight," Troy said, as Martin turned off and headed down Eighth Street. "We might even need your help, you down?

"Yeah. You know I'm not wit' no cruddy ass niggahs. What do you need me to do?"

Troy thought for a second before answering. "Page Martin and tell him to meet you on Fourth and Kalhoun about one tonight. Me and Maurice will be waiting to ambush his ass."

"Cool," Emmit replied.

As Troy walked away he thought about his brother, Seth. *This hit is strictly for you, bro.*

Young Assassin

❋ ❋ ❋

Maurice reached for the cordless phone on the floor and dialed Lemar's number. He put it to his ear, hearing it ring twice before being answered.

"Hello."

"Hi, Alvina. Is Lemar there?"

"He's sleep," Alvina said. "Do you want me to wake him up?"

"No, that's okay, just tell him I called."

"I will. Hey, Maurice?"

"Yeah?"

"Have you talked to your parents today?"

"No, why?"

"Well, I was just wondering if your mother told you that the house on Milburn Street is being put up for sale," she replied. "Your brother just bought a brand new five bedroom house out in Virginia, and we're all moving in."

Maurice smiled. "Really?"

"Yes, really."

"When is this supposed to happen?"

"I'm not sure, but it'll probably be after your niece or nephew is born," Alvina said.

"Oh, congratulations, y'all didn't even tell me."

She yawned into the phone and apologized. "We were gonna tell the family at the same time."

"Okay, Alvina. Tell my brother I called."

"Goodnight, Uncle Maurice."

He put the phone on the table in front of him, as his pager sounded. He unclipped it from the pocket of his shorts and looked at the number. It was Troy. He reached for the phone again and dialed the number.

"Maurice?" Troy's said, sounding strange.

"What's up, Troy?" Maurice asked.

"Meet me on the Avenue in twenty minutes."

"What's the matter?"

"I can't discuss it over the phone. There's something really important I have to tell you."

"Troy, I'm chillin' and I don't feel like moving," Maurice said. "Can't you come over here?"

"Maurice, meet me on the Avenue in twenty minutes," Troy said again. "And believe me, what I have to tell you will be worth you moving."

As Maurice heard the dial tone, he put the phone down and sighed.

❄ ❄ ❄

Emmit jogged upstairs as soon as he got home, grabbed the phone, and took it into his sister's room. He turned on her lamp and dialed Martin's pager number and put in his phone number. He smiled, as he sat on his sister's unmade bed, waiting for Martin to call him back. *I thought Martin Reed was a cool dude*, he thought.

That fact that he'd snitched on Lemar and Seth was one thing, but now he was trying to blackmail Lemar, and that was beyond cruddy to Emmitt. Especially where Maurice was concerned, which was the only reason he was even setting Martin up in the first place. He respected Maurice, and felt that he needed the help. *What goes around, sure does comes around*, Emmit thought.

A minute later, the phone rang.

"Hello."

"Emmit, you beep me, man?" Martin said.

"Martin, I just got robbed on Peabody Street," Emmit lied. "I need to buy the same amount, quick."

There was a short pause. "Give me a minute," Martin replied. "I gotta go to Northeast, and meet up with this dude."

"A'ight, man," Emmit said. "Do you think you can meet me on Fourth and Kalhoun Avenue about one?"

"Yeah, that's cool. Your ass better be there too. Don't be wasting my time."

"I will." Emmit hung up the phone, walked out of his sister's room and went back out.

After buying a dime bag of weed, Troy went to the liquor store to buy a blunt and a small bottle of whiskey. As he drove his car down the block, he drank half the bottle, instantly feeling tipsy. He decided to park the car on Kalhoun Avenue, to roll up the blulnt, and fire it up.

Thirty minutes later, he walked down the Avenue, constantly touching his lips. Troy had reached a high like never before. *Damn, what was in that shit,* he thought, as a strange feeling overwhelmed his body. He stopped and stood underneath a tree full of leaves, and watched the cars go up and down the Avenue, with his eyes barely open.

"Hey, Troy!" a voice called from somewhere nearby.

He turned in all directions in slow motion, and saw Maurice crossing the Avenue diagonally. Troy's smile became bigger as his friend approached.

Maurice scratched the top of his head, as he stepped onto the curb. He walked toward Troy and looked at him strangely. "Okay, fool, what's so important?"

"You, Lemar and Martin Reed," Troy said.

Maurice looked confused. "What?"

"Do you remember Martin Reed?"

"Yeah, what about him?"

"I spoke to Lemar today after getting a job at his place, and he told me that Martin blackmailed him into giving him a job as a chef," Troy explained. "He's been working there for awhile. I saw him at Lemar's bistro today myself." He looked at Maurice, who still had a confused looked on his face. "Martin claims to have witnessed you killing Officer Bailey. He told Lemar that if he didn't give him a job, he was gonna snitch on you," he poked Maurice in the chest with his pinkie finger, "as the murder suspect."

Maurice frowned and shook his head. "There's always something," he said, looking away. He turned back around to face Troy. "I wonder why Lemar never told me?"

"Because D.C.P.D. is on you like flies sticking to shit. He doesn't want you to get locked up," Troy replied. "He knows I was gonna tell you. Do you think Martin is lying?" He pulled his .38 from his hip.

"Whether he's lying or not isn't important," Maurice said. "He already crossed Lemar once before, so that niggah's gotta be dealt with."

"And he had the nerve to show his face around here after what he did to Lemar and Seth," Troy said, gripping the handle of his gun.

Maurice looked down at the weapon in Troy's hand. "I can't believe he told Lemar that he'll snitch on me. To be honest, I believe Martin wants to die."

"Well, let's give him what he wants. We got the opportunity to get him tonight," Troy told him. "I saw Emmit, get out of some truck Martin was driving a little while ago. I let him in on everything, and he's gonna set Martin's ass up. Both of them should be on Fourth and Kalhoun in a few hours."

"Man, I haven't killed anybody in a while, and I thought I wouldn't have any more reasons to kill again." Maurice sighed. "But it looks like I got a number of reasons to kill Martin."

"So, I'll tell you what. Let's get in my ride, drive to Fourth Street and wait for him."

"What was he driving?" Maurice asked.

"A burgundy Ford Bronco," Troy responded.

They started walking up the block at a slow pace. Maurice looked up at the dark sky, seeing the moon hide itself behind the smoky clouds. *It was three years ago, around this same time, that I killed my first victim, and now three years later, it appears I'm gonna kill my last,* he thought.

❊   ❊   ❊

Martin headed back Uptown, a couple of thousands of dollars richer. Hustling was much easier than cooking food. He hadn't realized how much he missed the streets, until he saw his stash growing. He looked out at the street before him, listening to music, with a half empty bottle of beer in between his legs. A few minutes later, he turned onto Kalhoun Avenue. He came to a stop at a red light, and looked at the time on his digital radio. Martin took a sip of beer and thought about Emmit. He looked at the black plastic bag on the floor, which had an ounce of crack cocaine in it, wishing he was at his apartment with one of his tricks, instead of coming back to meet up with somebody who couldn't handle himself.

Troy and Maurice sat in the car, looking across the street at Emmit standing on the corner, waiting for Martin to show up. Troy drank the last few swallows of his whiskey and gripped the gun in his lap. He screwed the top back on the bottle and looked at Maurice.

"You ready?" he asked.

"More like anxious," Maurice replied.

Emmit moved around nervously, up and down the street. His adrenaline doubled, once he saw beaming headlights coming toward him. When the truck pulled over to the curb, Emmit braced himself, as the window rolled down, and Martin appeared behind the glass. He looked across the street, and saw Troy and Maurice slowly getting out of their car.

"Get in," Martin said. "The door's open."

Emmit looked at him. "Just toss me the stuff," he said. "I'm in a rush."

"Well, give me the money then, fool," Martin replied.

"I'll be right back," Emmit said, taking off like he was at a track meet. He glanced back after he got a few yards away, and noticed Martin looking at him strangely.

Suddenly, gun shots rang out.

Emmit instantly turned around, and saw Martin slowly crawling out his truck onto the ground, squealing like a pig. Maurice and Troy looked like soldiers, as they stood over Martin with their guns drawn.

"What the fuck is this shit?" Martin asked, looking up at two gun barrels.

"This is for what you did to Seth and Lemar," Troy said, smiling as he stumbled a bit.

"You drunk motherfucka, what do you think you're doing?" Martin asked, looking up at Troy.

"Busting some caps in your punk ass!" Maurice replied. "Didn't your dumb ass know that what you told my brother would reach my ears?" Maurice fired two rounds straight to his temple. He looked down at Martin's body. "One less niggah,"

"Let's go!" Troy shouted to him, as both of them ran back across the street to his car.

Young Assassin

Emmit looked around, to see if anybody had just witnessed the cold-blooded murder. Suddenly, he saw a middle-aged black man sitting on the porch of a bricked townhouse. The man stared back at him for a few seconds, before getting up and rushing into the house.

"Shit," Emmit said out loud. "That could be trouble."

❋ ❋ ❋

Officer Casey sat behind a booth on the first floor of the Fourth District Precinct. She immediately hung up the phone and rushed out of her seat. She ran up two flights of stairs, bumping into several police officers, before she reached her destination.

"Yes, Officer, what is it? Another tip on a case?" Detective Sanders asked.

"It's much bigger than a tip, Detective," she replied, out of breath. "There's been a murder at Fourth and Kalhoun. The killing appears to be drug related." She was so excited that she hurried to swallow. "A man who lives near the location witnessed the entire thing."

Sanders looked at her. "Officer, that's nothing new. Do you know how many murders I have on my hands right now, and how many witnesses have backed out or disappeared?"

"Well, Officer Brown, who's at the scene, said the witness told police there were two suspects, and one of them was identified as Maurice Patterson."

A smile appeared on the detective's lips. "Well, in that case, this is wonderful news," he said. He got his keys from his desk and quickly threw his suit jacket on. He turned out the overhead lights and headed out into the hallway.

Casey grinned, as she walked next to him. "Sir, it looks like we can finally pin something on Maurice."

"Officer, go down to the courthouse and get a warrant for Maurice's arrest I want to be ready to arrest his ass, as soon as I come from the crime scene. Also, send a few squad cars to the Patterson house to see if he's there."

❀ ❀ ❀

Detective Sanders stood on the 1700 block of Kalhoun Avenue, talking with the man who had witnessed Martin Reed's murder. Sanders and a few other officers had searched the Ford Bronco, and came across large sums of money in the glove, and cocaine on the floor of the front seat.

"Are you certain it was Maurice Patterson?" he asked the witness.

"Yes sir," the man said. "I know his face and know who he is. He and other youngsters around here sell drugs all over this Avenue."

"Okay, sir, what exactly did you see?" Sanders questioned. The witness gave the police information concerning the murder, and said Maurice Patterson's name repeatedly.

"Did you recognize the other gunman?"

"I've seen him around here a lot. I think he lives down on the 1600 block."

"You have any idea exactly where?"

"No, I don't, sir."

"What kind of car were Maurice and the other gunman in?"

"An old blue or black Pontiac Grandville with a white rag or convertible top."

"Okay, what is your name, sir?"

"My name is David Turner."

"Well, Mister Turner, would you please come down to the station with me and describe what the other gunman looks like so our artist can draw a sketch?"

"Certainly, detective."

Chapter Twenty-Three

Lemar paced through his bistro, angry that Martin was not there on a busy day, especially when he was scheduled to work. He'd called Martin's house several times, but there was no answer.

He walked through the swinging door of the kitchen, and yelled to the other cooks. "Where the hell is Martin?"

Just then, a short, chubby Latino guy walked up to Lemar. "Hey, amigo, I guess you haven't read the paper or watched the news?"

Lemar frowned. "What?"

"Martin was killed last night. It said on the news that your brother and another guy from his crew were suspects."

Lemar sighed. "Damn!" he yelled. He looked away from the cook, and noticed that everybody in the kitchen was looking at him. "What are all of you looking at? Get back to work! There are people out there waiting to be served!"

He sighed again, and walked back out to the dining area. It looked as if Lemar had seen a ghost, when he saw Troy going behind the bar. Lemar shook his head, and walked toward him.

"Troy, why?" Lemar asked.

"Why what?" Troy asked, looking at Lemar.

"Don't play dumb with me."

"Look, we had to send him away," Troy replied.

"Why did you get Maurice involved? I thought you were gonna handle it yourself?"

"Maurice had a right to know, and after I told him about what was going on, he wanted to get Martin more than I did."

"Well, in case you don't know, the police are already looking for you and Maurice," Lemar said, taking a seat at the bar.

"I already know."

"Well, if you know, then what the hell are you doing here?"

"Because, I have a job to do."

"Look, Troy, you gotta leave now. I can't have any drama up in my spot."

Troy sighed. "Okay, I'll leave. But if you don't mind, I need to fix me a drink first."

Lemar looked at him as he stood up. "Sure, go ahead."

After Troy had his cocktail, he headed out and drove to the playground on Tilden Place.

Troy thought about his life, as he stood on the sidewalk outside the rec center. He'd read the paper and looked at the news, and wondered if Maurice knew they were wanted. He had been so set on paying Martin back for what he did to Seth, that now he was about to join his brother at the overcrowded D.C. jail.

He looked around the playground that he'd been coming to since he was a kid. He reached into his back pocket for a blunt, and he walked to his car. He ignited the engine, put his headlights on, and drove away slowly.

Troy wondered why things had to be this way. J.B. had managed to move on with his life by joining the Air Force. Keith had put the gangsta life behind him, and settled down a bit. And just when he was about to take his brother's advice and take time out to do something more positive and constructive with his life, he became a wanted man for murder one.

Twenty minutes later, Troy came to a traffic light in downtown D.C. He looked across the street at a young light-skinned woman standing outside a liquor store. She appeared to be looking at him. Troy admired her curves in the light blue dress she wore.

He pulled over and motioned for her to come to the car. As she walked, her breasts bounced up and down, which immediately turned him on. His mouth watered, as he looked at her like a slab of beef. When she approached him, he reached across the seat and opened the door. The woman got into his car, closed the door and smiled at him.

"So, how are you tonight?" she asked.

Troy eyed her up and down three times before answering. "Fine, and you?"

"I'm okay, honey. Just doing what I have to do to pay the bills," she said. "What you wanna do?"

"Something triple X rated," Troy replied.

"Do you have at least fifty?"

"Fifty dollars? Yeah, of course," he said.

"Well, drive two blocks and turn into the parking garage," she said. "By the way, my name is Juicy Lucy and yours?"

"I'm Troy."

Lucy held out a hand in front of his face. "The money," she said, as he drove the way she'd indicated.

Troy reached in his back pocket, and pulled out a fresh hundred dollar bill. Lucy took it, smiled, and reached inside her pocketbook. All of a sudden, her left hand grabbed a hold of his collar as she grabbed a metal object with her other hand. It was handcuffs. She had slapped them on him so fast, he didn't even know what had happened.

"Stop the car!" she said to him, in a rude tone.

Troy stopped the car and looked at her. "You're a cop?"

"That's correct, you freak. You're under arrest!" She pulled a dispatch radio from her purse. "Calling all units. This is Tucker with a suspect I busted on L Street Northwest. We just entered the parking garage on the 1500 block. I repeat, this is Tucker with a suspect I busted trying to buy sex on L Street Northwest."

"Copy, Officer Tucker," a voice came back over the radio.

Young Assassin

"This is Unit B-One-One-Six. We'll be right there."

Troy cursed silently, as he eyed the woman with a look of deadliness, knowing that he'd just removed himself from society forever.

❈   ❈   ❈

"I don't want to be a burden to you," Maurice said, sitting on the floor of Emmit's basement. "I just didn't have anywhere else to hide out. I think I should go." He stood on his feet.

Emmit stood up as well. "They might have another police car in the alley, so be careful. They've got cops all over the city looking for you."

"How would they know where to look?" Maurice asked.

"Are you joking? They know everything about the K.A.M., especially you," Emmit answered.

"Something doesn't add up," Maurice said thoughtfully. "Either someone dropped a dime, or someone's been following me."

"Or the police know enough about us to know where to look," Emmit responded. "They know where you hang out."

"Well, I'm gonna leave," Maurice said.

Emmit ran upstairs and Maurice followed. When they got to the living room, Emmit motioned for Maurice to stay back. He walked toward the living room window and peeked from behind the curtains, seeing a second police squad car pulling up behind Officer Casey.

"What's out there?" Maurice asked anxiously.

"Shit, it's the police," Emmit said, as he pushed the curtains back. "I bet all the extra cops are gonna watch the backyard." Emmit ran to the den and looked out into the backyard. "If you're gonna leave, it has to be now."

Maurice walked toward the back door. Just as Emmit opened it, he saw another squad car moving slowly up the alley. They looked at each other for a few seconds, before Emmit shut the door. They peeked through the window, and saw the vehicle move at a snail's pace past the backyard, until it turned off at the end of the alley. Emmit turned the knob and opened the back door again.

"Okay," Emmit said. "I'm gonna make sure the other two cars are still out front. I'll be back." Emmit hurried back to the living room, and saw the squad car behind Officer Casey pulling off. "Okay, go!" he yelled out to Maurice.

As he looked out the window, he saw Maurice hopping over the fence in the backyard, and sprinting up the alley.

Maurice watched the third squad car exit the alley, and turn left down the block. He hurried, looking behind him, hoping the second squad car wouldn't enter the alley from the other end until he was clearly out of sight. He knew he couldn't go home, not even to get a few things. If the cops were watching anybody he ever hung around, he knew for sure they were camped outside of his mother's house. Lemar was also out of the question.

Walking at a fast pace, he peeped in the direction of Keith's block, and saw a police car parked in front of his house. He thought about stealing Keith's old Mazada minivan that he always parked a block away, but Maurice knew his car was hot, and his best bet was to be on foot.

After he took a few steps, Maurice turned back around to look at the police car again. Suddenly, the police car backed down the street in a terrorizing acceleration. As the car slammed on brakes, Maurice kept his calm.

"Sir, stop and put your hands up!" a female voice said, through the patrol car's intercom.

As soon as he saw the officer behind the wheel get on her CB radio, his fast walk turned into a brutal sprint down Seventh

Street. Racing down the sidewalk as fast he could, he looked behind him, hearing sirens the entire time. He was nearly struck by a car as he ran out into the crosswalk on Sheridan Street, but he rolled over the hood and kept moving. He thought about trying to escape down a nearby alley, but alleys were always a good way to get caught. He felt the best way to avoid capture was to flat outrun them.

He ran down Sheridan Street for two more blocks then headed up Fourth Street. By the time he got to North Dakota Avenue, Maurice's speed began to slow down. Officer Casey drove ahead of him, and turned sharply into the street to block him off. Maurice's momentum carried him directly into the passenger side door, making him collide against it and fall instantly. As soon as he got to his feet, another squad car was there, blocking him off at another angle.

Officer Casey got out her police car, and shot a couple rounds into the sky. Gasping for air, Maurice threw his hands up. He looked at the two officers with their guns drawn, as he felt Officer Casey place her soft hands on his shoulders.

"Maurice, why did you make us chase you?" she asked.

"No reason," he came back. "I just felt like running."

"Maurice Patterson, you're under arrest for the murder of Martin Reed," Officer Casey said, with a smile. "You have the right to remain silent. Anything you say will be used against you in a court of law. You have a right to an attorney. If you can not afford an attorney, one will be appointed to you."

As a group of squad cars showed up on the scene, Officer Casey placed Maurice's hands behind his back, as the other two officers kept their Glocks in his direction.

As he felt the familiar handcuffs clutching his wrists, Maurice took a deep breath.

"Damn," he uttered.

Chapter Twenty-Four

On an unbelievably warm February afternoon, Tia walked
through the hustlers and pushers on Eureka Street, on her way
back to her old neighborhood.

After walking to the front of her building, she walked up a
flight of stairs to her mother's apartment. She immediately
noticed that the door to her mother's place was ajar. She slowly
pushed it open and stepped inside, feeling the heat rush across
her face. She covered her nose, as a foul smell lingered in the air.
The place was entirely empty, as if her mother had sold everything she had. All she saw were a few framed pictures of her
brother on the floor, along with a bunch of soiled toilet paper.
She walked through the apartment, and stopped at the kitchen at
a slapping sound.

Tia turned and saw a scrawny woman holding a crack pipe
sitting on the floor. She wore a dingy bra and no panties, expos-
ing her bushy vagina.

Tia looked at the woman and put her hands in the pockets of
her leather coat. "Where's Bonita?" she asked.

"In her room," the strange woman said. "You got some rock?
You smokin'?"

Tia gazed at the woman, turned and walked toward her mother's bedroom. When she entered, she saw her lying on the floor,
snuggled underneath a pink wool blanket with her eyes closed.

"Mom," she said.

Bonita opened her eyes partially. "Tia?" she asked, instantly sitting up. "Where the heck you been? Do you get high?"

Tia gave her an awkward frown. "Ma'ma, please come with me so you can get help."

"I don't need help." Bonita stood up, removed the blanket, revealing her stained T-shirt and dirty pink underwear.

"Please, Ma'ma!" Tia pleaded. "Please come with me so you can get better."

"I don't wanna get treated, Tia! I wanna get high!" Bonita shouted.

"Momma, your mind is so gone that you can't even remember to lock your door in a neighborhood like this. And who's the naked girl in the kitchen? Is she a prostitute?"

"Leave my house, Tia," she ordered.

"No, listen to me." Tia placed a hand on top of Bonita's head, feeling the tangles of her dyed blonde hair. "Don't go out like this."

"All I care about is crack. It's all I ever think about. So if that's the way I'm going out, I'm fine wit' dat."

Tears ran down Tia's face. "You're givin' up on yourself, Ma'ma. There are so many people who were addicted to crack, who managed to get clean and get on with their lives."

"Please go," Bonita said. "I'm not gonna say it again."

Teary-eyed, Tia looked at her mother and walked out the apartment.

❊   ❊   ❊

Detective Sanders and the two officials assigned by the Judicial Court walked up to the residence of David Turner and stood on the porch, waiting for the door to be answered.

by Mike G

Detective Sanders looked back at the traffic coming up and down the somewhat trouble-free Kalhoun Avenue, wondering whether Maurice being locked up was the primary reason. A minute passed, and he decided to knock again.

"Look," one of the officials said, pointing to a stack of newspapers that was piled up on the porch by a cart.

"It doesn't look like Mr. Turner's been here for a while," Sanders said. He knocked again, as two women wearing fake fur coats came out of the house next door.

"Excuse me," Sanders said to the ladies, as he walked over to the railing that divided the porches. "I'm Detective Sanders, District of Columbia Police Department," he said, flashing his badge. "I was wondering if you've seen Mr. Turner around?"

"I haven't seen David since Christmas," one of the ladies said. "But his car has been parked outside his house the entire time." The woman pointed to a white Hyundai Excel. "It hasn't moved in months."

Sanders looked at the woman, then gazed back at the front door.

"Maybe he's not home," the older agent said. "Maybe we should try back tomorrow."

The detective frowned as he turned around to face the women. "Have you seen anyone on his property since you last saw him?"

"No, sir."

"I have a feeling something is not right here. Did you know that Mr. Turner is supposed to testify in a very big homicide case?"

"Yes, he told me about it on Thanksgiving when I had him over for dinner."

Sanders had heard enough. He turned to face the door, and reached in his holster that was strapped around his rib cage, retrieving his .38 revolver. "Stand back and plug your ears every one." He took a few steps back, as he aimed for the lock on the front door, cocked the hammer three times, and blasted the lock. He kicked in the door, making it swing wide open into the wall.

As he looked down at the large amount of mail on the floor by the doorway, he instantly smelled a foul odor, unlike anything he'd ever smelled before.

"Mr. Turner?" he called loudly. "David?"

The two agents followed him inside. Sanders looked all around the main floor of the house, with his gun drawn. "He hasn't been picking up his mail either," Sanders said. "Like I said, something isn't right." He turned on a lamp in the living room and looked around. "You two stay right there," he told the agents.

He slowly walked around until he saw a room that appeared to lead to a den. As he entered, the odor became almost unbearable. The room was very dark, so he searched the walls for a light switch, and bumped into what he thought was a cocktail table. Eventually he found a switch and turned it on.

As he looked around, he saw a man slumped over on a black loveseat decorated with roses. Sanders frowned, as the handle of a screwdriver hung out of his right temple.

Sanders cursed under his breath as he walked slowly toward the man and lifted his head. He closed his eyes, and shook his head, as he gently placed the man's head down and walked back to the living room. The two agents were pinching their noses to keep from smelling the gruesome stench, when Sanders returned.

"Everything okay, Detective Sanders?" the agent asked.

"No, everything isn't okay," Sanders responded. "Another witness has been murdered."

by Mike G

Officer Reynolds stood behind the counter of the Fourth District Precinct, squeezing the telephone receiver as tightly as he could. His blood boiled, as he wondered what could be done about Maurice. After Officer Bailey's death, and the monumental task of retiring Lemar Patterson from the drug game, he knew things hadn't gotten any better. With the arrival of Maurice, things had actually gotten much worse. Over a three year period, Maurice had been a murder suspect so many times, that an office pool was going around to see how many murders Maurice was going to commit before getting caught.

He headed to the second floor. When he got there, he entered a small room where Officer Brown and a few rookies waited for him. He looked at them and drew his weapon. He placed the gun down on the table, and pounded his fist inside his palm. The three policemen looked at him, and then one of the rookies spoke up.

"Reynolds, what's the matter?" the rookie asked.

"Maurice Patterson is getting off once again!" he shouted. "I just got a call from my Captain, saying that some government agents told him they found David Turner dead inside his home a little while ago. Maurice has beaten the Reed case. Damn! Anyone who's down for killing Maurice, say I!"

Brown raised his hand. "I," he said softly. "This shit has to end."

"The justice system in this country is worthless," a rookie said aloud. "There's only one way Maurice will stop his shit, and that's if we make him stop. Count me in."

Reynolds and the two other officers looked at the first rookie. "And you?"

"I don't like him either," the first rookie said. "At the end of the day, all I want to do is go home. Fuck Maurice. Let's bury the fucker!"

"Unanimous," Reynolds said. He looked at his fellow officers. "If Maurice comes back to his neighborhood without as much as a conviction, we will put him six feet under. Do I make myself clear?"

Officer Brown frowned as he nodded. "Agreed," he said.

❊   ❊   ❊

Maurice smiled to himself, as he squinted his eyes inside the dimmed room within the confines of the overcrowded D.C. jail. He sat behind a table next to Ryan Dalby, waiting for lawyers to arrive. Ryan had informed Maurice a week ago that executives from the prosecuting attorney's office were looking to cut him a deal. Although Ryan knew Maurice wouldn't be the least bit interested in a plea bargain, he was interested in what they had to say.

Ten minutes later, Ryan looked at his watch, as two correctional officers opened the door. A sharp dressed black man, in an expensive gray suit, along with an elegantly dressed Latino woman, walked in behind them. As Maurice looked at the pair while they seated themselves at the table, he turned to Ryan. His lawyer watched as the man and woman placed their briefcases on the table and looked in his direction. Ryan turned to meet Maurice's gaze, then extended his hand across the table.

"I'm Ryan Dalby, Maurice's attorney," he said to them.

"I'm Assistant U.S. Attorney Zachary Eweing," the man said, extending his hand. "Along with me is prosecutor and public official, Lydia Garcia."

Ryan shook her hand and looked towards Zachary Eweing. "You said something about a deal," he said, getting to the point.

Eweing looked in Maurice's direction. "Maurice, as you know the Reed case was dropped against you after a witness was found murdered. We couldn't hold your co-defendant, Troy Cummings, after the charges were dropped. But there's Officer William Bailey and Calvin Sparks' cases left."

"You don't have anything on my client in either of those cases," Ryan interrupted. "Nothing at all. The judge is on the verge of dismissing the Bailey case altogether. In three years, the U.S. Attorney's Office and D.C.P.D. have found no leads, no witnesses, nothing!"

Lydia Garcia smiled towards Ryan, and for the first time spoke up. "We'll drop the charges in the Sparks case, because it's too difficult to prosecute Maurice for a crime that we can't prove he committed."

"What are you offering in the Bailey case, murder two?" Ryan asked. "Thanks, but no thanks. We'll take our chances in court."

"You're not understanding me," Garcia said. "We'll drop the charges in the Sparks case altogether, and the charges in the Bailey case against Maurice can be melted down to third degree murder."

"We're talking seven years tops," Eweing added, looking at Ryan sternly. "Mr. Patterson can be out of prison by the new millennium or soon afterwards. We just want him off the streets now."

Ryan looked at both of them and sat up. "Now that's a bargain that you don't see everyday."

"No, it isn't," Garcia responded, with a straight face. "So, do we have a deal, counselor?"

"You want my client behind bars so bad that you'll..."

Maurice touched Ryan's shoulder and cut him off. He thought about what was in store for him if he returned to the streets so soon. Maybe someone would try and pay him back, and if not now, then someday. He thought back to his string of victims. Some of them deserved to die and experience the pain that he'd put on them, but he knew a few of them didn't. He recalled the perpetual twisting and turning of his soul over the course of the three years prior to his latest arrest. Accepting this plea was the least he could do, to try and hold on to whatever soul he had left.

"I'll take it," Maurice said, standing up.

"Maurice, no!" Ryan advised. "You're a winner here. You can beat this if you want to. They don't have anything…"

"Shut up, Ryan," Maurice ordered, cutting him off. "I said I'd take it."

Ryan shook his head and took a deep breath. "My client is not thinking. He should get credit for any days he's served in the past," he said and stood up. "If you can agree to that, then we have a deal."

Eweing placed his hands on the table and looked at Ryan. "Seven years minus ten months," he said, as if meditating on it. "All right. We have a deal, counselor."

❄ ❄ ❄

When Lemar went to see Maurice the next day, he found his little brother sitting in a small lounge, guarded by an overgrown D.C. correctional officer. Maurice smiled when he saw him. He placed his hands in his pockets and walked toward Lemar. The two brothers embraced.

Usually visitors weren't allowed in this area of the facility, but Maurice had asked a guard to do him a favor.

"What are you doing here?" Maurice asked.

"Maurice, I came to apologize to you."

"Apologize?" he asked. "What for?"

"I blame myself for what happened to you," Lemar told him. "When I started hustling back in the day, I didn't know the impact it would have on you. I was only thinking about myself, and all the money I could make. I should've been more aware of how it would affect you. I know you made your choice to mess with the streets, but I could've been a better big brother to you then I was. I could've been a better man altogether."

Maurice smiled. He had never known Lemar to have regrets about much, and he'd never known him to talk like this.

"Thanks for the apology, but it's really all my fault," Maurice said. "Like you said, I made the choice to mess with the streets. The choice was mine and mine alone." Maurice looked at the prison walls. "This is where it ultimately got me."

"I'm sorry, little brother."

"All of that doesn't even matter now," Maurice said, slapping Lemar on the back. "What's done is done."

Lemar nodded. "I guess you're right," he said, placing his arm around Maurice. "But I still feel it's my fault that you're here. I feel like I'm to blame for what happened to you when you were on the outside. And when I first learned of your activities, I should've tried to turn you away from it."

Maurice smiled. "It falls on me," he said. "Just like you made the choice to be a hustler, I made the choice to be a hoodlum. Even if you had never hustled, there's no guarantee that I would've never fired a Mac-11. I've done a lot of cruddy things in my life like having Veronica stabbed and that old man killed. It's not like you told me to do any of that stuff. Look, I understand what you're saying, and I'm even touched by it, but please don't blame yourself for how I ended up."

The room filled itself with silence, as Maurice stepped away from Lemar and looked at the wall for a moment. As he scratched his chin, he turned back around to look at his older brother.

Young Assassin

"I still say it's my fault," Lemar said to him sincerely. "I don't believe for one second that what I was into didn't have an impact on you, because we both know that it did. It's good you're trying to own up to your wrongdoings, but it's my fault, and no matter how much you try to convince me that it isn't, we both know that it is."

Chapter Twenty-Five

Two months later, Emmit rode his black mountain bike up
and down Kalhoun Avenue, seeing the Neighborhood Watch
patrolling on foot up and down the street. There wasn't a crack
pusher in sight, or any crackheads strolling up and down the
Avenue. Since Maurice's plea, the Police Chief vowed to clean
up the streets.

Indeed, it was time to give the community what it wanted.
There are other ways to live life, he thought. Most of the original
hustlers and thugs were either locked up or dead, and that
lifestyle was beginning to play itself out.

He rode by a sewer on Third and Kalhoun and reached into
the pockets of his sweatpants. He looked up into the sky, thinking, *the only time you should even begin to sell drugs is when
there's no other way*. He felt it was time to be either a laid-back
hood or no hood at all. He grabbed the sixty dollars of crack
cocaine from his pocket and reluctantly tossed it down the sewer.

Tia held both of her children's hands as she entered through
the doors of the D.C. jail on a Sunday evening. That day there
were very few people visiting inmates. She walked toward the
glass window, showed her ID and signed into the log book.

Young Assassin

Since the last time Tia saw Maurice, she'd heard that he'd been in and out of jail. Although she hadn't been with him since the day she told him of her pregnancy and eventual abortion, Tia was curious to see if there was anything that could be salvaged between them.

She was lead to a glass booth with a phone receiver next to it on the sixth floor. She took a seat, and placed both of her children on her lap as she waited. From where she sat, she saw Maurice approaching slowly from a back room. He held a nonchalant expression, as he sat down and picked up the receiver on the other side of the glass.

"Hey Maurice," she called.

Maurice looked at her with a straight face. "Tia."

"How've you been?"

"Look, we haven't talked in a long time," Maurice said. "So, what's this all about?" He looked down towards her two children, then back up at her.

"I don't blame you for being angry with me, even now," she said to him. "I'm sorry."

"Sorry isn't gonna bring Brian back. Sorry isn't gonna bring back our son or daughter you destroyed either."

"Maurice, please," Tia said, looking into his eyes. "I've always loved you."

"Brian was becoming a very good friend. What you did was beyond cruddy."

"And I told you why he had to die," Tia whispered.

"Tia, this isn't the time or place to be talking about that," he responded.

Tia burst into tears. "My brother sold crack to my mother, Maurice. His own mother!"

Maurice looked at her, and tears fell on the steel desk. He took a deep breath. "How's Bonita?"

Tia looked away as she wiped her tears, and took a moment to get herself together. "She overdosed and died two weeks ago," she replied, her face full of anguish.

"I'm so sorry to hear that," Maurice said, looking down at her kids. He focused on Donovan, and remembered when Tia was pregnant with him in school.

"Who's the small one?" Maurice asked, as he pointed to her youngest child.

"This is Antonio," Tia said. "I was pregnant with him when I last saw you."

Maurice forced himself to smile.

"Did you hear about Troy?" Tia asked.

"No, I didn't. What happened?"

Tia looked away. "He's locked up out in P.G.County."

"For what?"

"Well, at first I heard he got locked up for soliciting a prostitute downtown. Then when he got out, he tried to rob somebody out in Maryland, but got caught. When the police searched him, they found two guns with hollow points in the clip. Now everybody is saying the police are charging him with Martin Reed's murder because those are the same type of bullets that was found in Martin's body, and at the scene.

"Damn." Maurice replied.

"Can I ask you something?" Tia asked.

"Yeah?"

"Is there ever a chance we can..."

"No," Maurice said, cutting her off. "I don't think we were meant for each other."

"I see," she said, surprised that he read her mind.

"But we can be friends."

Tia smiled. "So, I hear you plea bargained. I'm surprised that you did."

"I had to. I have my reasons, but I really don't want to talk about it."

"Okay, fine. I guess there isn't much more to say. I just wanted to see you again. She placed her hand on the window. Bye," she whispered.

Maurice started at her empty chair for a few seconds, before returning to his cell.

❋　❋　❋

Maurice stood in the small courtroom in front of the bench, as the judge went over the case paperwork. He was oblivious to the countless number of police officers crammed in the courtroom. Ryan stood beside him, going through paperwork of his own, as he waited for the judge to finish.

Maurice's gaze shifted to the side of the courtroom, where he saw his father holding his mother closely. Alvina and Lemar were located in the next row. He gave his brother a slight head nod to let him know that he would be okay. As Maurice went to turn his attention back to the judge, he saw Bam sitting in his wheelchair by an opened door.

Niggah, you better be glad I don't have a gun, Maurice thought.

Over to the side, Lydia Garcia stood patiently with her hands behind her back. When she turned and saw Maurice looking at her, she smiled slightly, then turned around to look in the direction of the judge.

The judge folded the papers she was reading, and looked toward Ryan. She hit the gavel on the bench twice and said, "Counsel may now approach with the prisoner."

When Ryan approached with Maurice, Garcia stepped forward also. After looking at Maurice for a few seconds, the judge eyed both Ryan and Garcia.

"Maurice Patterson, you have entered a guilty plea of Third Degree Murder in the death of D.C. Police Officer William Bailey. Today, the Court sentences you to six years in prison, which is to be served at the District of Columbia Correctional Facility."

The judge slammed the gavel on the bench. As Maurice turned to look in the direction of his family, a correctional officer put his hands behind his back. As he was led down the aisle of the courtroom towards the entrance, he saw Ryan walking beside him

Suddenly, Ryan pointed ahead at a uniformed police officer pulling a gun from his holster. Maurice looked and saw Officer Reynolds charging towards him with his weapon drawn. Before the correctional officer could put the handcuffs on Maurice's wrists, Maurice broke free and reached quickly for the officer's automatic pistol.

Suddenly, two shots were fired at Maurice, hitting him in the shoulder. Within seconds, numerous police officers had their weapons drawn in response to the commotion.

Maurice fired two shots of own as he closed the gap between him and Reynolds, hitting the officer in the stomach. Maurice displayed a slight grin, as he watched the bold policeman fall to his knees, holding his stomach with both hands. Officer Reynolds displayed a distraught look as he managed to fire several more shots. Three bullets struck Maurice. Two in his chest and one in the side of his neck.

"Maurice!" Alvina screamed from somewhere in the court-room.

Maurice looked up towards the ceiling, holding his neck as blood gushed through his fingers. Lemar finally fought his way through the screaming crowd, and knelt down beside his little brother.

Young Assassin

"I'ma cold beast," Maurice managed to say. "Did I get that niggah?"

Lemar looked over at Reynolds, who had passed out on the floor. *I think you did*, Lemar thought.

Suddenly, Maurice felt a familiar calm. A feeling he hadn't experienced since the kidnapping incident. Then the calm turned into a disturbing peace as his head turned.

"Somebody get an ambulance!" Lemar yelled. "Hold on Maurice! Don't die on me, man!"

But it was too late. Maurice Patterson was dead.